THE SILENT GUEST

SALLY RIGBY

Storm

Ebook ISBN: 978-1-80508-683-3
Paperback ISBN: 978-1-80508-684-0

Cover design: Lisa Horton
Cover images: Trevillion, Shutterstock

Published by Storm Publishing.
For further information, visit:
www.stormpublishing.co

ALSO BY SALLY RIGBY

A Cornwall Murder Mystery

The Lost Girls of Penzance

The Hidden Graves of St Ives

Murder at Land's End

The Camborne Killings

Death at Porthcurno Cove

The Marazion Murders

Cavendish & Walker Series

Deadly Games

Fatal Justice

Death Track

Lethal Secret

Last Breath

Final Verdict

Ritual Demise

Mortal Remains

Silent Graves

Kill Shot

Dark Secrets

Broken Screams

Death's Shadow

Detective Sebastian Clifford Series

Web of Lies

Speak No Evil

Never Too Late

Hidden From Sight

Fear the Truth

Wake the Past

Question of Guilt

PART ONE

THE SETUP

ONE

VIVIENNE

Sunday

'Don't sit there, Lola, sweetheart,' I say to my five-year-old daughter as she's about to jump on the sofa. I've spent ages making sure the cushions are just right and don't want her to mess them up. 'Come over here and help me get everything ready.'

I shake my head. Am I being silly? Doing all this because I have someone arriving for an interview. It's not me who's on show here. Well... it is, I suppose, and it's making me nervous. I hate the thought of someone thinking I can't even manage my own home.

The reason for all this is that a housesitter is due to arrive shortly to discuss staying here and looking after Willow, our crazy labradoodle, when we go away next weekend. Willow hates going to kennels, and after the last time – when she came back with a large cut on her nose because another dog had bitten her – I'd felt so guilty that I promised her she wouldn't have to go again. Okay, promising a dog something sounds ridiculous, but I swear she understands me. Except I've been so busy at work that the family party coming up totally slipped my mind and I haven't done anything about finding someone to look after her. So this is all very much last minute.

It was my husband, Miles, who'd suggested contacting Pet & Home Watch because someone he works with uses them and they recommended a sitter called Amelia. I checked the site, and I couldn't believe she was available on the date I wanted. The trouble was she only had one review, but one friend's personal recommendation is far better than lots of reviews from people we don't know. Anyway, I ended up submitting a request for her services and she accepted, which means I won't have to miss my family party.

Today's more a chance for us to get to know each other, rather than an interview. That doesn't make it any easier, though. What if she doesn't like me? Or she thinks the place is a mess? She could put up a bad review about me on the website. It's not just sitters who get reviewed; if she says anything bad, I won't be able to use the site again and—

Stop it.

The house is fine. It's clean and tidy… Well, as much as it can be with a small child and a dog. And it's not like she's going to inspect all the rooms and go into the cupboards.

But what if she wants to take a tour? My body tenses. I'm being ridiculous and need to get over myself.

The doorbell rings, jolting me from my thoughts, and my heart skips a beat.

'The lady's here, Mummy,' Lola says excitedly, running out of the lounge into the large square hall of our Victorian house.

I smooth down my shirt, hurry to the front door and open it.

Standing there is Amelia, her smile warm and inviting. She's the spitting image of her photo on the website, albeit not as tall as I'd expected. She's quite petite, actually, with a vulnerable attractiveness about her. I stare at her dark pixie haircut with envy. My features are far too heavy to suit a style like that.

'Mrs Campbell?' she asks with a friendly tilt of her head.

'Yes, but please call me Vivienne. Do come in. This is Lola.' I gesture to my daughter, who's pushing herself in front of me.

'Hello,' Lola says, smiling in that endearing way of hers. It never ceases to remind me how precious she is.

'Hello, Lola,' Amelia replies, walking into our home. 'It's so good to meet you. Is Willow here?' Amelia bends down slightly, looking around as if expecting the dog to come bounding in.

'She's in the garden because Mummy wanted to keep everywhere tidy for you,' Lola announces innocently.

My insides clench with embarrassment, but I force myself to remain cool.

'Well, it is housework day,' I say with a forced laugh and a wave of my hand, trying to appear nonchalant, though I'm anything but.

'I totally get it. I'm the same,' Amelia says with a grin that lights up her face.

Amelia's easy-going nature seems to fill the house, and I let out a sigh of relief. My trepidation was for nothing. It's going to be okay. Then again, I do spend my entire life overthinking things – even if I try to hide that part of me from other people.

'Come on through to the kitchen and I'll put the kettle on. Is coffee okay? Or something else if you'd rather? Um... we've got tea, water, squash?' I add.

'Coffee would be lovely, thanks,' Amelia responds. 'I don't suppose you have any oat milk, do you?'

'Yes, I do. My husband prefers it, and so do I now.'

I hadn't even considered that she might want ordinary milk. Thank goodness she didn't.

When we reach the kitchen, I hurriedly scan the room and notice a dirty cup on the side. Damn. I'd forgotten to put it in the dishwasher. I also spot the half-empty bottle of red wine beside the fridge, left over from last night when I'd had a couple of glasses with my dinner. I should've put it away in case she thinks I'm a big drinker. I'm not.

'Take a seat.' I gesture towards the tall chairs around the island.

Amelia pulls one out and sits down.

'Can I sit next to you?' Lola asks, standing very close to our guest and staring up at her.

'Why don't you go outside and play with Willow? It's such a nice day,' I suggest. 'You'll be bored listening to the grown-ups talk.'

'I want to stay here,' Lola says, her bottom lip jutting out and her feet planted firmly on the floor.

The thing about Lola is she's five going on fifteen, and always in the thick of it, asking questions non-stop. It's because she's so bright, and of course, I'm proud of her. But it can be exhausting. Miles finds it cute, but he's not here all the time because his job takes him away a lot. He's a civilian pilot for the army, which means he gets to travel all over the world, but could end up being in some dangerous situations. He loves his job, but it's hard for us; we hardly ever get to see him and I'm always worrying that something will happen and he won't come home. Because his missions are secret, I never know where he is or when he'll be back.

I love my daughter deeply, but juggling childcare with Miles's absence and my job as an accountant isn't for the faint-hearted. Sometimes, it feels like I might as well be a single-parent family.

But – and this is a big but – the money Miles earns is good, and he's promised it's only until he turns fifty. Then he's going to retire and we can have some fun. That's another fifteen years, though, which seems interminable.

'It's fine. I don't mind if she sits here,' Amelia says with a reassuring nod.

Lola gives me a self-satisfied smile and climbs up onto one

of the chairs. I can't help chuckling, but I quickly turn my back to make the coffee because if she realises that her behaviour amuses me, she'll be even worse.

'I go to school and I'm in Mrs Robinson's class,' Lola says, looking up at Amelia.

'That's nice,' Amelia says. 'Do you like school?'

'Yes. But I don't like school dinners, so Mummy lets me take my own lunch.'

'Lucky you. I used to hate school lunches too,' Amelia says, nodding her agreement.

'Daddy bought me two lunchboxes, which I use,' Lola says.

'We alternate them,' I say. 'The unicorn one on Mondays, Wednesdays and Fridays. And the rainbow one on Tuesdays and Thursdays. Lola's very particular about it.'

'I'm not surprised – they sound amazing,' Amelia replies.

'I'll show you,' Lola says, jumping off the stool and heading round the other side of the island, where she pulls out her two lunchboxes.

'Wow... They're so cool,' Amelia says. 'I bet all your friends are jealous.'

'Yes. They are.' Lola gives a smug smile.

'Why don't you put them back and let me talk to Amelia?' I say.

'Okay, Mummy.'

I can't believe it when Lola does as I ask without moaning. Clearly, Amelia is a good influence. After replacing them, Lola climbs back up on the stool next to Amelia.

'Why don't you tell me about your housesitting experience?' I ask, placing two mugs of coffee on the island and sitting down opposite Amelia. 'I saw on the website that you haven't many listings of previous jobs.'

Damn. I hadn't planned on starting with that. Will she think I'm being critical?

Amelia nods slowly, as if agreeing with me. 'Yes, according

to the site, it does look like that. But that's because I haven't been registered with them for long. I've done private work. That's why I was so pleased when you chose me.'

At least she doesn't seem offended by my question.

'You were recommended by my husband's colleague – I don't know their name,' I say with a shrug, hoping she doesn't think badly of me not finding out exactly who had recommended her, given as she's going to be left in charge of our house. 'Also, I needed someone at short notice and you were available... It was fate,' I add, with a smile.

'Totally,' Amelia agrees, her tone light. 'I love animals and staying in people's homes. I'll look after your place as if it were my own. Promise. You won't even know I've been here when you get back. Like I said, I've done private housesitting before, mainly for friends and acquaintances. Just not through Pet & Home Watch – but they take references before our profiles are loaded to the site, so you can trust me,' she adds solemnly.

'Yes, of course. I'm sure I can,' I reassure her.

And I do trust her. Sometimes you can just tell with a person whether they're genuine or not.

'What time would you like me here on Friday?' Amelia asks, taking out her phone and glancing at me.

'I'd like to leave late Friday afternoon, after work. It's only ninety minutes from Winchester, but you know what the traffic can be like at the weekend. I'm aiming to arrive by seven to seven-thirty, so I think leaving at five should give us enough time. Does that work for you? We'll be back sometime Sunday afternoon.'

'No problem. I'll leave work early. Is quarter to five okay for the handover?' Amelia asks while typing into her phone, presumably putting the time into her calendar.

'Perfect. But I don't want to get you in trouble for leaving before you're meant to.'

Otherwise, she won't want to housesit again – assuming that

this weekend works out, and I'm pretty sure it will. I have a good feeling about it.

'Oh, don't worry. I'll work through lunch,' Amelia says with a dismissive wave of her hand. 'My manager won't mind. She's very flexible.'

Amelia returns the phone to her handbag and picks up the mug in two hands. She takes a sip of coffee while looking in my direction, as if expecting me to ask something else.

'So... what do you do?'

'Oh, I work in a charity shop,' Amelia replies, her fingers brushing the side of her nose.

No wedding ring. Does that mean she's single? Is it rude to ask? Of course it is.

'In Weeke? That must be very rewarding.' I wince, sounding trite even to myself.

'It has its moments,' Amelia says with a sigh. 'What are you planning to do while you're away?'

Clearly she doesn't wish to talk about it, or she wouldn't have changed the subject.

'My aunt and uncle are throwing a ruby wedding anniversary party on Saturday. It's just Lola and me because my husband's working.'

'Daddy flies planes,' Lola joins in. 'But it's secret,' she adds, her eyes shining as she brings her finger up to her lips.

'That sounds very exciting,' Amelia says, interest flickering in her eyes.

'But not so exciting for us,' I say, laughing lightly and tucking a loose strand of hair behind my ear. 'He's a pilot with the army and is away *a lot*.'

Oh, God, stop prattling on. Amelia doesn't want your life story.

'I'm sure it can't be easy. Is there anything else you want to know about me and my experience?' Amelia asks, leaning forwards eagerly.

'No... I think we've covered everything.' I smile.

'Okay, well, next Friday it is. What about meeting Willow?' Amelia asks as she gets off the stool.

Of course. The main reason she's here. How could I forget that?

'Yes, I was about to suggest we go into the garden so you can see her.'

I lead the way to the back door.

'What sort of dog is she?' Amelia enquires as she follows me.

'She's a labradoodle. That means she is a bit Labrador and a bit poodle,' Lola answers.

'I'm sure she's adorable,' Amelia responds as we step outside.

I exchange a glance with her over the top of Lola's head and we both smile. Amelia's nice. I really like her. Even though she seems a bit younger than me, maybe in time we could become friends. It's been ages since I had someone genuine to talk to.

Willow comes bounding over and sniffs Amelia, who doesn't seem to mind muddy paws and nose on her jeans.

'Do you have a dog?' Lola asks.

'No, but I'd love one.' Amelia sighs while patting Willow.

'Why don't you?' Lola asks.

'Lola, stop bombarding Amelia with questions,' I say, giving an apologetic shrug.

'I don't mind. It's because I work full-time and so does my partner,' Amelia replies. 'It's not good to leave dogs alone all day long.'

Ah, a partner. There is someone.

'Mummy works,' Lola says with a frown.

'But often from home,' I add, not wanting Amelia to think that Willow is left alone all the time.

'That makes it easier. Unfortunately, I can't do that with my job,' Amelia says, smiling at Lola.

'What about your children?' Lola asks.

A shadow crosses Amelia's face. 'I don't have any.'

'Why not?' Lola continues.

'I'm sorry,' I quickly say to Amelia, hoping she's not annoyed at the intrusive questions.

'It's fine,' Amelia says. 'I get asked this all the time by family. You know how it is.'

I want to know more, but it's not my business. Maybe she wants children but can't have any. Anyway, it's nothing to do with me.

'Yes, family can be thoughtless.' I nod. 'Lola, throw the ball for Willow so Amelia can see how good she is at fetching.'

'Okay.'

Lola picks up the ball from the ground and throws. It doesn't go far, but Willow makes a crazy leap at it and we all laugh.

'I think this is going to work out really well,' I say, relief washing over me.

'So do I,' Amelia agrees. 'So do I.'

TWO

AMELIA

Friday

'Here goes nothing,' I mutter.

I've parked a little down the street from her house, and my hands grip the steering wheel tightly as I psyche myself up to leave the car. I walk, turning into the driveway of the large Victorian red-brick house that's going to be mine for the weekend. The house looms before me, a stark contrast to our two-up-two-down terraced property.

The fancy silver Mercedes is standing there with the back open. My eyes narrow.

It's all right for some.

Before I even have time to walk to the front door, it opens and the little girl comes running over, her feet pounding on the ground. Her mother is only a few steps behind, her movements tense and hurried.

'Sorry I'm late,' I say, stepping forward. 'We had a problem with the computer at work and I couldn't leave.'

Not quite the truth, but who cares? She thinks I work at a charity shop, so she can hardly complain.

In reality, I'm a data-entry clerk for a Winchester-based pensions company. It makes me yawn even thinking about it. There was no reason for me not to have been here on time, but where's the fun in that?

'No problem. It's only a few minutes after five,' Vivienne says, a smile plastered on her face. But it doesn't quite reach her eyes, which are tight and anxious. She's wound up tighter than a screw. I bet she thought I wasn't going to turn up. 'Are you okay sorting everything out yourself? I've left detailed instructions. We really need to get going... you know, because of the traffic.'

'Of course,' I reassure her.

'Where's your car?' Vivienne asks.

'I parked it on the street. I didn't want to block you in.'

I walk with her back to the house, my steps brisk and purposeful, and then step to the side as she wheels out a rather large designer suitcase.

Vivienne looks at it, and then at me. 'Yeah, I know. It's ridiculous. We're only away for two nights, but there's always so much to take. You know what it's like with kids.'

'No. I don't have any,' I say, putting a slight chill into my voice.

'Oh, I'm sorry. I forgot.' Guilt flashes across Vivienne's face.

'Forget it,' I say lightly. 'You get going.'

Despite her outward appearance of being in control, I can already see that she's easy to wind up. A bit pathetic, but useful to know.

'Right, okay. Willow's food's in the utility room. The instructions I've left you include looking after her, when to take her out, how much to feed her, etc, etc. And here are the house keys.' She hands over a set with a Mercedes keyring. 'Your room's upstairs, the first on the left.'

'It's next to mine,' Lola says, hopping from foot to foot, her pigtails bouncing with each movement.

What's wrong with this kid? I've yet to see her standing still. Too many E-numbers or something else?

'That's nice,' I say, forcing a smile and reaching out to ruffle her hair. But she pulls back, her face scrunching up in displeasure.

'Lola hates her hair being touched. She's almost obsessive about it,' Vivienne says apologetically, her eyes darting between me and her daughter. 'Although I do get it, I hate people touching my hair, too.'

'Sorry, Lola. Am I forgiven?' I ask the little girl, my tone saccharine sweet.

God, if I had a child who acted like that, I'd send her back. Clearly the woman can't control her and thinks her behaviour's endearing. Newsflash: it isn't. The child would soon shape up if she lived with me.

'Okaaay,' Lola whines, her voice grating on my nerves.

I draw in a deep breath. Willing myself to calm down. They'll be gone soon.

'We'll see you when we get back on Sunday afternoon,' Vivienne says, heading towards the car. Her steps are hurried; she's clearly eager to escape, and I have no desire to delay her further. 'I'm not sure exactly what time it'll be, but I'll be in touch to let you know when we're on our way.'

'Okay. Now you two have fun, and don't worry, everything will be fine here. Promise,' I say, in my best enthusiastic voice while, of course, crossing my fingers behind my back.

'I'm not sure about fun – it's more a duty visit,' Vivienne says with a grimace. 'But it will be good to get away, and Lola's excited about seeing the family because we don't meet up often. Oh yes, I forgot to say, if you go into the garden, watch out for the well in the rear corner beside the hedge. There's a low fence around it to stop Willow and Lola from accidentally falling in, but it's very deep. I keep meaning to get it covered, but haven't yet got around to it. Anyway, Willow's outside. There are towels in the utility room for you to wipe her feet, because she's bound to get muddy – it's like she does it deliberately, and—'

'Go, go,' I say, interrupting her, fed up listening to the endless instructions, treating me as if I'm a child. My patience's wearing thin. 'You'll be even later if you don't. Everything's going to be fine. You two enjoy yourselves and I'll see you when you get back. I look forward to hearing all about it.'

Seriously, what a worry-arse. How the hell does the husband put up with it? But of course he doesn't, because he's away flying all the time. Who can blame him? She's enough to drive anyone to distraction. I suppress the chuckle that's threatening to erupt from inside of me.

Vivienne seems to take the hint, because they climb into the car. Now she's taking ages strapping the child into her seat because she's wriggling around so much. It's like the woman only has two speeds: slow and stop.

Finally, they're ready and she drives away. I stand on the doorstep, waving enthusiastically in their direction, until the car can no longer be seen.

Dropping my arm, I turn and head into the house, inhaling deeply. The space is already familiar from the interview, but not as familiar as it's going to become. For now, it's all mine and I intend to make the most of my time here.

I walk straight to the kitchen, my fingers running along the cool marble worktop. My movements are purposeful and my mind's racing with a million and one possibilities.

What shall I do first?

Because now I'm alone, I can do what I like, and this is going to be fun. I glance out the window and see the dog playing in the garden. She's a cutie, even if she did make a mess all over my jeans the other day with her muddy paws and nose. It annoyed me that Vivienne thought it was funny. She could've offered to wash them.

Willow can stay outside for a bit while I get my bearings. I wasn't lying about wanting a dog but it not being possible. We had one at home when I was growing up, but she died when I was ten and— I force the memory out of my mind. Even after all these years, it's hard to face.

Anyway, dog-sitting isn't the real reason I'm here.

I want to get inside a home where I can do what I want with no one there to stop me.

The power's intoxicating.

But first things first. I have a call to make. My fingers twitch with anticipation as I reach for my phone and key in the number.

THREE

VIVIENNE

'I like Amelia. She's really nice, isn't she, Mummy?' Lola says to me from over the back seat.

'Yes, darling, she is,' I reply, my brow furrowing slightly. 'But I don't know… Do you think maybe we should've stayed a bit longer to make sure she was okay?' Especially as I thought I saw a strange look on her face as I drove away. But I'm not a hundred per cent. It could've been the light playing tricks.

I look in the rear-view mirror and see my daughter playing with one of her dolls. She's not really listening. I feel guilty about leaving so abruptly, but I needed to get going, and we're already hitting the traffic. Exactly what I didn't want to happen. It's Amelia's fault by arriving late, not mine, that I couldn't stay longer.

I drum my fingers on the steering wheel. Have I remembered everything? I know the suitcase is full, but most of it belongs to Lola. Her special pillow, toys, clothes and toiletries. I wasn't sure what to wear, so have brought a few different outfits with me.

I sigh softly. I wish Miles was here. But at least it means we can now have some photos taken. When he's with us, we don't because Miles is camera shy. He said it's linked to something called scopophobia – which is a fear of being looked at or seen. I'd never heard of it before.

You'd never think he has this problem when meeting him. He's the epitome of tall, dark and handsome – and so charming, too. Okay, so I'm more than a little biased. But that's what he's like. I still have to pinch myself sometimes that he chose me.

Miles said his problem started when he was a young kid, and his mum sent his photo to a modelling agency. They used him in commercials. He said he hated photos being taken over and over again and having to stand there after being put in different positions. And then being told it wasn't right. Even at our wedding, he wouldn't have one taken.

We got married at a registry office in the Lake District. Neither of us wanted a big wedding. Most of his family live in Canada and wouldn't have come over, and my family are up north and I seldom see them. We didn't even tell people until after the event. The lakes were a beautiful setting, and it was perfect. Even if there are no photos... Well, apart from the ones I took on my phone when he wasn't looking. I didn't think there was any harm in that. But he doesn't know. They're just for me to look at.

I take loads of photos of Lola and explain to Miles that we don't want her to end up with his phobia. She's too young to realise that there are none of me and her daddy.

My thoughts race back to leaving Amelia alone at home. It's only for a weekend and it's not like she wasn't recommended to us. There won't be any problems.

I glance again in my rear-view mirror at the back seat. Lola is still playing with her doll. 'Is everything okay back there?' I ask.

'Tammy's wearing her new dress,' Lola answers, holding up her doll proudly.

'That's wonderful, darling. How many different outfits did you bring for her?'

'Oh, just a few,' she replies casually. 'I want to make sure there's something to choose from in case I change my mind.'

I tense. Is she copying my behaviour? Worrying about everything? Surely not. I make a concerted effort to appear strong and sure of myself in front of everyone, including my daughter. I can't have her picking up on my little idiosyncrasies, even if inside there are times when I'm all over the place.

My mind goes back to the house, and I take a deep breath, trying to calm myself. I'm sure Amelia's going to be fine, and Willow seemed to like her, and vice versa. Seriously, I need to stop worrying. I'm going to enjoy the weekend away. It's going to be fun. It's natural to feel a bit uneasy when there's a stranger in your house. But everything's tidy. What if she starts going through all my drawers and everything? No. I'll be able to tell. Everything has its correct place.

'I think Tammy's going to have so much fun, sweetheart— Oh my goodness.'

'What is it, Mummy?' Lola exclaims, her eyes wide.

I grip the steering wheel tighter, my knuckles whitening. 'Look at the traffic. It's going to take us ages. The M3 is such a pain.' I sigh heavily, then try to put on a cheerful tone. 'Oh well, never mind. We'll get there eventually, and it'll be nice to see everyone. I hope we don't ruin anything by being late.'

'You've got to be relaxed and laid-back,' Lola says.

'Where did you get that from?' I ask, tilting my head slightly at her grown-up response.

'That's what Daddy says to you. Just be laid-back,' she explains.

A small smile tugs at my lips. 'That's a very good suggestion.'

'Does it mean you have to lie on the sofa? Or on the bed?' Lola asks, her brow furrowing in confusion.

'No, darling.' I chuckle. 'It means I should be more relaxed and enjoy things. And that's what I'm going to do this weekend. We'll have a great time and I won't worry about Willow and Amelia because they're going to be fine.'

I take another deep breath, trying to convince myself as much as Lola. Despite my anxiety, I'm determined to make this a memorable trip for both of us. If only this weird feeling would disappear... Then again, I'm used to unsettling feelings. It's been the story of my life.

The traffic crawls forwards at a snail's pace. I should have messaged my aunt before we left to let her know we might be late.

'Mummy, can we play I spy?' Lola asks, breaking through my thoughts.

'Of course we can, sweetheart. You go first,' I say, welcoming the distraction.

'I spy with my little eye, something beginning with... C.'

I scan our surroundings, grateful for something else to focus on. 'Is it... car?'

'No.' She giggles. 'Try again.'

'Cloud?'

'Nope.'

'Hmm... Is it your coat?'

'No, Mummy. It's the cat in the car next to us.'

I glance over to see a cat ornament dangling from the rear-view mirror of the car in the lane next to us. 'Oh, how clever you are. I didn't notice it.'

The game continues, and I find myself relaxing. It's amazing how children can pull you out of your own head sometimes. I remember my mum playing this with me on long car journeys, though, to be honest, we never went anywhere particularly exciting. At least not in my mind. Historical manor houses are not for the young to enjoy.

'Your turn, Mummy.'

'Okay, let me think...' I pause, scanning the road ahead. 'I spy with my little eye, something beginning with *L*.'

'Is it lorry?'

'No, but good guess.'

'Is it... lights?'

'Yes. The traffic lights up ahead. Well done, darling.'

As we inch forward, I notice Lola's reflection in the mirror. She's holding her doll close, whispering something to it. Sometimes I wonder what goes through her head, what stories she's creating. Miles says she gets her imagination from me, but I think she's far more creative than I ever was. I wouldn't be working as an accountant if I had real creative flair. But my choice was based on it being a safe option, after everything I'd been through.

'Did you remember to pack Mr Snuggles?' I ask, suddenly thinking of her favourite bedtime elephant.

'Yes – he's in my special bag,' she says.

The stuffed toy has been everywhere with her since she was two. I remember the panic when we thought we'd left him at a service station on the way to Cornwall last year. Miles had turned the car around and driven twenty miles back, only to find Mr Snuggles had slipped down the side of Lola's car seat the whole time.

The traffic starts moving a bit faster now, and the tension leaves my shoulders. I check the time. We're only going to be about forty minutes late. Not too bad, considering.

'Look, Mummy.' Lola points excitedly out the window. 'That cloud looks like Willow.'

I glance up through the windscreen at the cloud formation she's spotted. It does look a bit like a dog, which makes me think of Willow back home with Amelia. I wonder if she's found where we keep the treats yet? It's all in the instructions I left, but knowing Willow, she'll probably lead Amelia right to them anyway. She's clever like that.

'You're right, it does look like Willow,' I agree. 'Do you think Willow and Amelia are having fun?'

'Of course,' Lola says with absolute certainty. 'Amelia said she loves dogs, and Willow looked happy when she stroked her. That means they're friends.'

I wish I had her confidence. But she's right. Willow doesn't usually take to strangers so quickly. Maybe that's a good sign. I try to hold on to that thought as we finally pass the worst of the traffic and pick up speed.

FOUR

AMELIA

Phone call made. Now I can have a good look around. And I mean *good*. Not the abridged version Vivienne gave me when I visited the other day. She rushed me around so quickly I could barely get my bearings. It was like she didn't want me to see anything but felt obliged to give me a tour, anyway. Which is weird when you think that she's handed over her house to me and I can go anywhere I want without her knowing.

But where to start?

Where might I find the most interesting stuff?

Her study?

Yes.

I'm still amazed that she didn't spend forever giving me minute by minute instructions, despite leaving an extensive list, before leaving for her weekend away. She's clearly the type to go on and on whatever the situation.

My footsteps are eerily silent on the polished hardwood floors as I head towards the study where she works. Even though she briefly showed me the room when she gave me a tour of the house, my heart is racing with a mix of excitement and trepidation. This has got to be the best part of 'housesitting':

the fact that I have total access to everything and have no idea what I'll find. Each room promises to reveal more secrets, and more glimpses into the woman's life. And as knowledge is power, the more I get to see, the better it will be.

I push open the door to her study and make a beeline for the tall oak bookcase. A person's reading material is a great place to start to find out more about them. I run my fingers along the spines of her books. The shelves are packed with self-help books, crime fiction and childcare books. An interesting combination, for sure.

On the top are several framed photos, all of her and her daughter. What was her name again? Lily? No, Lola. I take one down and study it intently. My insides clench at the sight of their smiling faces. Does she deserve to be so happy? No way.

What about the husband? Where's his photo? Vivienne mentioned he works for the army as a pilot... but does he? And is that even a job? I reckon he doesn't even exist, because from what I've seen so far, there's no sign of him. It wouldn't surprise me if he was a figment of her imagination, because she thinks it makes her seem more respectable. Except the child mentioned him, too. But she's only five, so what does she know?

I turn my attention to the large antique desk in the centre of the room. There's a laptop sitting right in the middle. Can I get in it? My palms grow sweaty as I approach, imagining all the secrets it might hold. I lift the lid, but it's password protected. Hardly surprising, but disappointment courses through me, nonetheless.

I exhale loudly.

Maybe the filing drawer will reveal something? I bet she keeps paper records of everything in case her laptop packs up and she loses everything. I open the bottom right-hand drawer, and in there are a set of dark green hanging files, all neatly labelled: *Bank, Medical, Credit Card Statements, Insurance,*

Dog, Home... You name it and it's got a folder. It's as if she's inviting me into her life.

Soon, I'll know everything there is to know about her and can plan my next move.

My mouth turns up in a broad smile as the thrill of power rushes through me.

Carefully, I begin sifting through some of the folders, my eyes drinking in every detail. There are medical records for both her and her daughter, but nothing for the mysterious husband. Lola has a history of respiratory issues. Poor girl... Wait, who am I kidding? I couldn't care less. It's not like she's dying or anything. I bet Vivienne's one of those overprotective mothers who takes her daughter to the doctor at the first sign of a sniffle.

The bank statements are interesting. Regular amounts paid in from the company where she works, but is it enough for the upkeep of this place? Old houses eat up the money. Maybe there really is a husband... Or he could be an ex-husband and this is all paid for through maintenance.

I replace everything exactly as I found it, not wanting to give the game away yet. That surprise will come later, when she least expects it.

My mind's buzzing with questions.

What else can I discover here?

There's got to be something interesting in the pristine kitchen. I leave the study and make my way there.

The surfaces gleam and are topped with a range of high-end appliances, like a fancy kettle and air-fryer. It's not fair that she has so many of these when all we can afford are the cheap versions.

The fridge contains organic vegetables and expensive cuts of meat – of course – and in the recycling, I spot two empty wine bottles. Does she drink alone? I wonder what the *husband* makes of that.

Leaving the kitchen and heading upstairs, the first room I

enter clearly belongs to the girl. It's so frilly, decorated mainly in pinks, and there are stuffed animals perched in every available space. It's like their glassy eyes follow me as I move around the bedroom inspecting it. Opening the closet, I run my hands over the tiny dresses and shoes. Again, way too much pink. Doesn't Vivienne know anything about gender stereotypes? Obviously not if this room is anything to go by. I roll my eyes. Don't get me wrong, I'm not a raging feminist, but even I know we don't want our kids to be throwbacks to the 1950s.

There's a small desk under the window and on there are colourful drawings and alphabet practice sheets. I bet Vivienne's one of those mothers who pushes her child to excel at everything. My fingers trace the wobbly letters, a strange feeling settling in my stomach.

I'm so desperate for a child, but Tom's still not ready. Will he ever be? Tears fill my eyes, and I hurriedly blink them away. This isn't the time to dwell on issues in my life. I have a job to do here.

The main bedroom is my next stop. Here, finally, I find evidence of the elusive husband. If you can call it evidence. In a mirrored wardrobe that runs along the entire side of one wall, there are men's clothes hanging neatly, with all the shirts together and then suits. They also appear to be colour coded. Bloody hell, he must be a right neat freak. I look in the set of three small drawers that are in the left-hand side of the wardrobe and in the top drawer are pairs of men's underwear, the second contains socks and the third belts. Again, all very evenly placed. But that doesn't mean he lives here on a full-time basis. He could be a visitor.

I open one of the other wardrobes, inhaling the scent of Vivienne's perfume that lingers on her clothes. My fingers trail over the soft fabrics, imagining her wearing them. All the hangers are identical and facing the same way, but unlike the men's clothes, these aren't organised in such a methodical way.

Moving on to the large en-suite bathroom, which has a free-standing Victorian bath in the centre that I plan to use later, there are more interesting finds. In the medicine cabinet, I discover a variety of pills. Some are prescription, others over the counter. Sleep aids, painkillers and, hidden right at the back, some anti-anxiety meds – I know this because I've been prescribed them in the past.

Is Vivienne battling demons?

If she is, it's nothing more than she deserves. Not to mention, it will make it even easier for me to carry out my plans.

I laugh out loud. The more I'm discovering about this woman, the more fun I envisage happening.

I pop into the guest room, where I'm to sleep. Like the rest of the house, everything is perfectly arranged. But knowing what I already do about the woman who lives here, it feels fake. Like it's all for show.

Completing my tour of the house, my head spins with all I've discovered. Vivienne Campbell's life appears perfect on the surface, but I'm convinced it's full of hidden depths and secrets. But whatever's lurking won't stay hidden for long. I'll make sure of that. That's a promise. And I don't feel a single ounce of guilt for what I'm about to do because the woman deserves it and nothing will persuade me otherwise.

Glancing at my watch, I realise it's time to feed Willow and settle in for an evening of Netflix. I head to the kitchen, a smile playing on my lips. Vivienne has no idea that I now own her life. I can't wait to see how this plays out when she returns.

FIVE

VIVIENNE

Saturday

I pace nervously around the unfamiliar hotel room, clutching my phone as I wait for Amelia to answer. It's only nine, but I've been up since six, unable to sleep. The rain outside splatters against the window, matching the erratic rhythm of my heartbeat. Finally, after what feels like an eternity, a voice comes through.

'Hello.'

'Hi, Amelia, it's me,' I say, my free hand fidgeting with the hem of my shirt. 'Sorry to disturb you so early.' I wince at the sound of my high-pitched, strained voice.

'What's the matter?' Amelia sounds concerned, which only makes me feel worse.

Am I overreacting? It's not something I can help.

I bet she thinks I'm checking up on her. Which I'm not. Okay, maybe I am.

'I felt awful because we left so quickly yesterday. I wanted to make sure everything's okay and there's nothing I've forgotten to tell you.' The words tumble out of my mouth. Will she believe that's all it is?

I walk to the window and peer out at the gloomy weather. The sky's a dull grey, and raindrops race down the glass. I follow their paths with my eyes, trying to distract myself from the gnawing anxiety in my gut.

Lola's playing happily on the floor with her toys, oblivious to my inner turmoil. Oh, how I long for those carefree days.

'You didn't forget anything, and it's all fine. Don't worry, I have everything under control.' Amelia's tone's reassuring, and I feel silly. 'Did you get there okay yesterday?'

'We were a bit late because of all the traffic,' I admit.

'I'm sorry, that was my fault for not getting here on time,' Amelia says, sounding contrite.

'Oh no, I don't want you to blame yourself,' I hastily reply, catching sight of my worried reflection in the window. 'I'm just phoning. You know. It's not because I don't trust you. If it all works out, we can use you again. It's just...' I trail off, unsure how to express my concerns without sounding completely neurotic.

'It's just what?' Amelia prompts.

I take a deep breath. 'When we left, I thought I saw a funny look on your face in the rear-view mirror. But maybe I'm imagining it.' As soon as the words leave my mouth, I regret them. Could I sound any more paranoid? Except if I don't ask it's going to bother me the whole time.

'How can you tell I had a funny look on my face from that distance?' Amelia's voice has an edge to it now, and I mentally kick myself.

'I'm sorry, I'm just overthinking. Miles always tells me off for that,' I backpedal. 'How's Willow doing?'

'Everything's fine,' Amelia says, her tone noticeably cooler. 'Willow's been fed. She's playing in the garden.'

My eyes widen in alarm. 'What? In this weather? It's pouring with rain,' I exclaim.

'It's fine here. But if the weather changes and she gets wet, I'll wipe her down with one of the towels in the utility room.'

'Oh yeah, okay,' I say, relief flooding through me. But then another worry pops into my head. 'But if it does start to rain, don't leave her out for too long because she does get a bit of arthritis sometimes and—'

'Vivienne, it's all good.' Amelia cuts me off, her voice sharp. 'You don't need to check up on me. Willow's fine. More than fine. We're getting on well together. Now, if that's everything, I've got to go. I'm going out shortly.'

I freeze, my hand gripping the phone tighter. 'What? You're going to leave Willow on her own?' I ask incredulously. 'Surely you're not going to do that? I mean...'

'I won't be out for long, but I do need a couple of bits. You didn't expect me to stay with her *every* minute of *every* day, did you?'

My mind races, trying to find a solution. I don't want to upset Amelia, but I can't bear the thought of Willow being left alone for a long time. 'No, no, it's fine if you need to pop out,' I say, wanting to sound calm. 'She doesn't like being left alone. I should have said something about that, but I didn't. I assumed that if you're housesitting, you'd be there.'

I run a hand through my hair, frustration building. What am I meant to do? I can hardly refuse to let her leave the house. Willow's okay on her own when I leave her for work, but that's only part-time. This is different, though, because she's probably already missing us and doesn't know Amelia.

'I promise she won't be left on her own for long. I'll take her for a walk first and that will tire her out,' Amelia explains, as if she's talking to a young child. 'Don't worry. You have a good time. What do you have planned today?'

'We're going out for brunch with some relatives that I haven't seen for ages and the party's this evening.'

'Right, well, you have fun and don't worry about me and Willow. I can always take Willow in the car if you'd rather?'

'No, don't do that – she doesn't travel well. She might be sick and I wouldn't want that in your car.'

'Okay. I promise not to leave her for long.'

I breathe a sigh of relief, my shoulders relaxing slightly. 'Sorry. Ignore me. And I'm sorry, too, for upsetting you before.'

'No problem,' Amelia says lightly. 'I totally understand. This is the first time you've used me. I'll see you tomorrow when you get home.'

I end the call and feel totally ridiculous for sounding so pathetic. I stare out of the rain-streaked window, wondering if I'd made the right decision in leaving Willow with Amelia. Did I overreact? Am I a terrible pet owner by leaving Willow? Or am I being an even worse person by checking up on the housesitter? I slump onto the bed and groan, covering my face with my hands.

The phone rings, and I see on the screen it's Miles. Just knowing he's at the end of the phone line relaxes me.

'Hello,' I say happily.

'Hi. I can't be long but wanted to check how you're both doing,' my husband says.

'Lola's next to me. I'll put the phone on speaker.' I turn to my daughter. 'It's Daddy.'

'Daddy,' Lola squeals.

'How's my favourite girl?' Miles asks.

'We're in a hotel. We're going out with Mummy's cousins for *brunch*,' Lola says, pronouncing it very carefully. 'That means it's breakfast and lunch mixed up together.'

'Sounds great,' Miles says with a chuckle. 'Is everything okay, Vivienne?' he asks.

'I called Amelia to check on Willow. You're going to think I'm crazy, but I have this feeling that something's not right.'

'Did Amelia say there was anything wrong?' Miles asks, sounding concerned.

'No,' I admit. 'But she's going out, and I'm worried about leaving Willow alone.'

'But she's used to that when you go to work.'

'Yes, but this is different because I'm not there to settle her. Willow might get anxious.'

'I'm sure everything will be okay. From what you've told me, Amelia seems responsible, and Willow's a good dog. It's only two days. Stop overthinking because it's not good for you.'

'Yes, Mummy. Stop overthinking,' Lola repeats.

I burst out laughing. 'Okay, you two, you've convinced me. I'm being silly.'

'It's not silly to care about Willow,' Miles reassures me. 'But try not to let it ruin your trip, okay? You're supposed to be relaxing.'

'You're right.'

'You enjoy your brunch and I'll try and call tomorrow. Bye, Lola. Love you,' Miles says.

'Bye, Daddy.'

'Bye, Viv. Love you, too. And remember – stop worrying. Willow will be fine.'

I take a deep breath. 'I know she will. I promise to relax and not worry. Be safe.'

I try to push aside any doubts, but as we get ready to leave, I can't help glancing at my phone, half expecting a call from Amelia. The nagging feeling that something isn't quite right lingers like a shadow at the edge of my consciousness. Being hypervigilant is something I've always struggled with. But I try to shake off the feeling, reminding myself that there's no reason to have these doubts. Amelia's more than capable and Willow's in good hands.

As we step out of the hotel into the drizzling rain, Lola splashes in a puddle. We walk to the car, her yellow raincoat a bright spot against the grey morning. I'll focus on her excitement instead of my worries about Willow. The way her face lit up when she saw the hotel room last night, how she immediately claimed the window seat as her 'special place' to arrange her dolls. These are the moments I should be treasuring.

'Mummy, will Cousin Gail be at brunch?' Lola asks, carefully stepping over another puddle as we reach the car.

'Yes, and Cousin Paul, too. You haven't seen them since you were little.' I help her into her car seat, making sure the straps are properly adjusted. 'They can't wait to see how much you've grown.'

'Will they remember me?'

'Of course they will. They always ask after you when I speak to them on the phone.' I close her door and slide into the driver's seat, checking my phone one last time. No messages from Amelia. That's good. She'd contact me if anything was wrong.

The satnav says it's only a fifteen-minute drive to the restaurant, but I leave extra early, just in case. Miles often teases me, saying I'm the only person he knows who considers being ten minutes early as 'cutting it close'.

'Mummy, can we get pancakes at brunch?' Lola asks.

'If they have them on the menu, definitely.' I smile at her in the mirror. 'What kind would you like?'

'Chocolate chip. No, blueberry. No, both.'

Her enthusiasm is contagious, and I find myself genuinely looking forward to brunch. Gail always puts me at ease. She's one of those people who can fill any silence with comfortable chatter, never making you feel pressured to contribute more than you want.

I park outside the restaurant, ten minutes early, of course. We go inside and I can see that Gail and Paul aren't here yet. I didn't expect them to be. Gail has always operated on what we jokingly call 'Gail Time' – always fifteen minutes later than everyone else.

'Look, Mummy, they have a fish tank,' Lola says, hurrying over to look at it.

'Don't lean on the glass, sweetheart. You'll scare the fish.' I reach for my phone again, then stop myself. No. I'm not going to check. I'm going to focus on this moment, on Lola's excitement, on catching up with family I haven't seen in too long.

The smell of coffee and bacon wafts over and my stomach growls, reminding me how hungry I am. A young waiter with a friendly smile walks over.

'Do you have a reservation?'

'Yes, under Gail Matthews. We're a bit early.'

'No problem. Would you like to sit at the table while you wait?'

I glance at Lola, who's still transfixed by the fish tank. 'Actually, could we stand here for a few minutes? My daughter seems quite taken with the fish.'

'Of course. Would you like me to tell you their names? The owner's kids named them all.'

As he points out Ferdinand the blue tang and Sparkles the angelfish to an enthralled Lola, I realise I haven't thought about Willow or Amelia for at least five minutes. Maybe Miles is right. I can learn to relax, even if it's only for small periods at a time.

I glance out of the window. The rain's stopped, and a weak sun is trying to break through the clouds. Sometimes a change in weather is all it takes to shift your perspective. I take a deep breath, inhaling the comforting restaurant smells, and decide that for the next hour at least, I'm going to try to be present in this moment, with my daughter, enjoying ourselves with our family.

I make a silent promise to myself: I'll enjoy this trip, but as soon as we get home, I'll make sure to give Willow extra love and attention. And maybe, just maybe, I'll learn to relax a little more the next time we go away.

SIX

AMELIA

'What the bloody hell is the woman thinking, checking up on me?' I mutter under my breath as I pace around Vivienne's immaculate lounge after our phone conversation. The large, clearly expensive Persian rug muffles my footsteps, but it doesn't quell the irritation bubbling inside me. Seriously, I've literally only been here one night. And as for not going out anywhere – it's a dog, not a child I'm looking after. Willow can be on her own for a while without anything bad happening. Not once during the interview, or in the *extensive* instructions that were left for me, did she say I'd be chained to the place the entire time.

Then again, she could've said whatever she liked because I wouldn't have taken any notice. I'll do whatever I want and she can't stop me.

I glance out the window at Willow, who's sniffing around the well-manicured garden. I spot the well that Vivienne mentioned at the far end, its weathered stone circle rising about twelve inches from the ground, covered in climbing ivy. There's a low decorative fence around the perimeter. It's rather gothic –

I like it, but I suppose it could be dangerous for children if they were able to climb it.

The sky's overcast and it's threatening to rain. With a sigh, I head to the back door and open it. 'Willow. Time to come in,' I call. The dog looks up, her tail wagging, and she trots towards me. She's actually a real cutie; I hadn't expected to like her so much. As she enters, I grab a towel from the nearby pile on the counter and wipe her paws. 'There you go. Can't have you trailing mud all over your owner's precious floors, can we?'

Once Willow's settled on her plush day bed – as opposed to the crate for nighttime sleeping and for any time she's left alone – I pick up my mug of coffee from next to the coffee machine. I could get used to this luxury. It tastes so much better than instant. But those coffee machines are ridiculously expensive. My fingers drum against the worktop as I take a sip.

I need to get into Vivienne's laptop because there's bound to be stuff on there she won't want anyone to see. But where's the bloody password?

With purposeful strides, I head to her study and sit myself down at her desk, placing my mug on a coaster to ensure I don't stain the wood.

I swivel from side to side in her mahogany captain's chair with worn dark green leather upholstery while trying to work out where the passwords are. I'm convinced they'll be written down somewhere – she's that type.

I pull open the filing drawer in her desk and start sifting through again, my fingers flicking past folder after folder. Then I notice a bright-blue plastic wallet right at the back in the last slot. I'd clearly missed it last night when I searched the drawer. But that's hardly surprising since the last few folders look empty.

My heart races as I pull out the wallet, its glossy surface smooth beneath my fingertips, and slide out the contents: three sheets of paper. My eyes widen as I realise what I've discovered.

'Yes,' I say, my voice echoing in the quiet room as I do a fist pump.

This is it. Everything I want to know. I now have complete access to her life.

I stare at the two pages of typewritten passwords and read everything that's both written and typed. Some passwords are in shorthand, but they're easy to work out.

Oh, Vivienne. You've made it so easy for me...

I scan the passwords for one relating to her laptop, but there's nothing on the first page. On the second, though, I spot what I'm looking for.

I open the laptop and the keys click softly as I type. Each sound sends a thrill through me. I press enter and... I'm in. The screen loads revealing a background photo of Vivienne, her daughter and the dog. Yet again, there's no husband. I really need to investigate that further, but first things first, let's look at her photos.

I click on the folder and scroll through all the images. Again there are only photos of her daughter, until I find a rear view of a man wearing a baseball hat holding the daughter's hand. Is that him? It could be anyone.

After finding nothing of interest in her photos, I navigate to her social media page. The posts are few and far between, and mostly reposts of someone's charity events or something equally mundane.

Vivienne Campbell must be the most boring person on this earth.

I move on to her email inbox to see if there's anything there to interest me, but my disappointment grows with each click. Literally, her emails are invoices and newsletters from mailing lists she's joined, mostly cooking and self-help.

This woman's more vanilla than vanilla.

I close the email inbox and lean back in the chair. The dark screen of the laptop reflects a mischievous glint in my eye as a plan begins to form in my mind.

I'm going to make her life less boring, and she won't even see it coming.

Standing up, I stretch out my arms above my head and swing them from side to side. My mind's already racing with possibilities.

The first thing I'm going to do is get a duplicate set of house keys cut. Then *mi casa, su casa* as they say, and she really will have something to worry about.

I giggle nervously to myself while closing the laptop, and carefully return everything to its original position. I don't want her to suspect anything. What's going to happen to her, she's going to blame on herself.

My heart pounds with excitement and a touch of nerves. I take a deep breath, inhaling the scent of lemon furniture polish that permeates the room.

I leave the study and return to the kitchen. Willow lifts her head, her tail thumping against the bed. 'Sorry, but I'm going out, so you'll have to go into the crate.'

After bribing the dog with treats to get her to obey me, I grab my denim jacket from a coat stand by the front door, the fabric rustling as I pull it on. My hand hovers over the house keys, hanging innocently on a hook. With a quick glance around the hall, as if expecting Vivienne to suddenly materialise in front of me, I pocket them.

Opening the front door, I take one last look around. Everything's in its place, neat and tidy, just as Vivienne had left it. But soon, perfect will be a thing of the past.

Before getting into Tom's car, I glance back at Vivienne's house. From the outside, it looks like any other large old fancy home. But that's where the similarity ends. Because inside, the seeds of discord have already been planted. And with careful nurturing, soon, very soon, they'll begin to grow.

I jump into the car and start the engine. With a beaming smile on my face, I drive out of the drive and head towards the city centre. I'm so preoccupied with thoughts of what I'm going to do that I don't notice the traffic lights have gone red until I've sailed right through them, narrowly missing a car heading towards me. They sound their horn loud and long, which gives me time to swerve, thankfully avoiding a nasty accident.

I give an apologetic wave and continue, the butterflies in my stomach working overtime and my breathing all over the place. After several minutes of careful driving and some deep breaths, finally I'm back on course. I allow my mind to go back to what I'm about to do. Getting my own set of her house keys.

Because this is only the beginning. I have plans, big plans. And poor, unsuspecting Vivienne has no idea what's coming. Well, it's no more than she deserves.

SEVEN

VIVIENNE

Sunday

The sun's setting as I pull into my driveway, park in front of the garage, and turn off the engine. Lola's fast asleep in her car seat, looking sweet and peaceful. She dropped off within minutes of us setting off, being exhausted from the late nights and non-stop activity. I sit still for a minute, watching her chest rise and fall, marvelling at how already she manages to take everything in her stride. I hope she stays like that and doesn't inherit my anxiety. Though why should she? It's not like my tendencies are based on genetics. If things hadn't happened the way they did, I might have been a completely different person.

Finally, I step out of the car and breathe in the evening air. A wave of comfort washes over me. I'm home.

We had a wonderful time at the anniversary party. It was so good to catch up with relatives I haven't seen in years. But it's wonderful to be back to the peace and quiet of home, where I can relax and feel safe. I bought the Victorian property ten years ago, with money inherited from my parents after they died in a boating accident. The moment I saw the warm red-brick property, with its decorative white-painted woodwork and sash windows, I fell in love. It was perfect. Miles felt the same when he moved in a few years later.

I stretch my arms out to the side, feeling a satisfying pop in my shoulders. As I lower them, my mind lurches back to the thought that's plagued me for much of the weekend. The one where I worry about everything being okay with Willow and that the house is all in one piece.

I laugh softly. 'Of course it's fine,' I reassure myself out loud, shaking my head at my own thoughts. It's not like we've been away for months. Nothing's going to happen over a single weekend.

I lift Lola out of the car and carry her to the front door, my feet crunching on the gravel. I stick my key in the lock and turn it.

'Hello,' I call out, stepping inside.

Silence greets me. That's weird.

'Hello?' I call again, my voice echoing through the empty hallway. Nothing. I head into the lounge and place Lola, who's still asleep, on the sofa and then walk to the back of the house and into the kitchen. Willow's in her crate, wagging her tail furiously, clearly pleased to see me.

'Hello, darling,' I coo, bending down to her level. 'How did it go? Did you have a nice time with Amelia?' My brow furrows as I look around. 'Where is she?'

I unlock the crate and let Willow out, giving her lots of fuss. She's crazy with excitement, her tail wagging so hard her whole body shakes.

'Do you need to go into the garden?' I ask, walking to the back door, opening it and letting her out.

I head back to the kitchen and scan the area. Nothing appears out of place.

My eyes land on the island, where I spot a note propped up against a jar of peanut butter. I walk over and pick it up.

Vivienne, thanks for the opportunity. I've left everything as I found it. Amelia xo

I stare at the words dancing in front of my eyes. Why has she gone? I thought we'd arranged for her to stay until we got back. What if we'd been delayed and Willow was left on her own?

I drop the note on the worktop and head outside to the car, my mind whirring with questions, to bring in the luggage.

Once everything's unloaded, I head back to the kitchen and look at the note again, shaking my head. Fiddling with the paper, I suddenly see more writing on the back.

P.S. Sorry I had to leave early. I couldn't wait. I have an early start tomorrow.

A frustrated sigh leaves my lips and I run a hand through my hair.

What the hell?

Okay, maybe we are later than I originally said. And I did forget to text to say that we'd left, but that was because I'd planned on being back around three or four. I hadn't realised there'd be so much traffic and roadworks. That's no excuse for her to take off. She could've phoned me to say... Then again, she could turn it back on me and say that I could've contacted her to say we were running late. Except, how can I do that while driving?

I hear Lola calling and hurry to the lounge.

'Hi, sweetheart,' I say softly, kneeling beside the sofa. 'Are you okay?'

Lola rubs her eyes sleepily. 'Are we home?'

'Yes, you were asleep for most of the journey. You were very tired.'

'Where's Amelia?' she asks, sitting up and looking around.

'She's gone,' I explain gently. 'She couldn't wait for us because she has work tomorrow and didn't want to be late home.'

I take Lola upstairs and give her a bath. The warm water seems to wake her up a little, and she splashes happily while telling me all about her favourite parts of the weekend. Once she's clean and dry, we settle down in her bedroom for me to read her a story. She yawns again. I hope she'll be okay by tomorrow for school. She can be a handful when she's tired and grumpy, which her teachers won't be happy about.

'Right,' I say after finishing the story and closing the book. 'It's time to go to sleep. I'm going downstairs to make your lunch for tomorrow.'

I always like to get it ready the evening before because it's such a rush in the morning getting both of us ready. During her first week at school, she'd had school lunches, but she didn't enjoy the food and asked to take her own lunch in like several others in the class. It's a pain, but what could I do? I don't want her to see school as a horrible place, so I agreed to try it for this year. Hopefully, she'll change her mind as she gets older and give me one less thing to worry about.

'Okay, Mummy,' Lola says, sounding so sleepy.

I smooth back her hair from her forehead. 'I love you, sweetheart.'

'Love you too, Mummy,' she murmurs, her eyelids fluttering a few times and then closing.

I move some of her toys from the bed and put them back where they're kept, and then head downstairs, still annoyed that Amelia left without bothering to speak to me. Well, if she wants me to add a reference to the housesitting site, she can think again.

I head downstairs to the kitchen and pour myself a much-needed glass of wine. With glass in hand, I walk to the back door to check on Willow, who's playing in the garden, running from one end to the other. It's as if she's hardly had any exercise over the weekend and she's having to get rid of all her pent-up energy. She certainly doesn't seem ready to come in, even though it's getting dark. As I watch her bound around, chasing shadows, I can't shake the feeling that something's a little off. Okay, so the house is exactly how I left it. But there's an intangible feeling hanging in the air that's making me uneasy.

Miles would tell me to stop worrying. That nothing's wrong and I'm only feeling guilty for leaving my home and pet in the hands of a relative stranger over the weekend. Logically, that does make sense. But he's not the one faced with this uncertainty that keeps nagging at the back of my mind.

EIGHT

AMELIA

Four weeks later

Monday

The last four weeks have gone by sooooo slowly, but finally the time has come for me to put my plans into practice. I couldn't risk starting sooner, as the culprit would be too obvious. But by now, Vivienne Campbell should have forgotten I even exist.

I lie in bed, a strip of morning light warming my skin. My eye twitches involuntarily, a tic I've had since childhood that worsens when I'm excited. A smile creeps across my face as I think about having taken this week off. Tom's already left for work, but not before making sure everything's okay. He gets me. More than anyone ever has in the past. And that's why I love him so much. I'd do anything for him. He deserves it.

I jump out of bed and head for the shower. The water pelts my skin, but I barely feel it. My mind's elsewhere, thinking of what's coming. Steam fills the bathroom as I stand there, imagining Vivienne's face when her life starts falling apart and she's helpless to stop it. My stomach clenches with anticipation.

I grab a quick coffee, the mug trembling slightly in my hand as I gulp it down. The bitter taste grounds me, helps me focus on the task ahead.

As I leave home, my heart races. It's not fear, though. It's excitement. The morning air is crisp as I step out of our terraced house. A few early commuters hurry past on the narrow pavement, heads down, absorbed in their own worlds. I walk to my car, which is parked on the other side of the road, and drive to Vivienne's house, parking a little down the road.

I'm close enough to see when she leaves. My eyes dart back and forth, scanning the street. I don't want anyone to notice me. A woman walks out of the front door of number twenty-three and onto the street. She passes the car with her Yorkshire terrier and I slouch down slightly, pretending to check my phone. She doesn't even glance my way. These people are so oblivious, wrapped up in their mundane little lives.

After a few minutes, Vivienne appears from her house. She's struggling with her daughter, who's being awkward. I'm not surprised. That girl's so spoilt. My lip curls in disgust as I watch the scene unfold. The girl – Lola, I remind myself – is throwing a tantrum about something. Probably her breakfast, or her clothes, or whatever insignificant thing has set her off this time. If she were mine…

But she's not. I tried talking to Tom again at the weekend about having a baby, but he's still not ready. Will he ever be? I get it, after what he's been through. But it doesn't make it any easier to deal with. The thought hardens my heart, fuelling my resolve. Life isn't fair. But Vivienne? She gets handed to her on a silver platter – the perfect house, the perfect family and by all accounts, the perfect husband. She doesn't deserve any of it.

Finally, the girl's in the car and Vivienne goes around to the front seat. I smile to myself, knowing from reading the schedule she keeps on her laptop that she'll drop the child off at school today and then head to Southampton for work. Monday morning there's always a staff meeting, so she doesn't work from home.

This means the house will be empty.

I sink down into the seat of my car as Vivienne drives past. There's no way she'll notice me, especially as she doesn't know what car I drive, but I hold my breath anyway. My hands grip the steering wheel so tight my knuckles turn white. Once they're out of sight, I begin counting to a hundred. In case she turns back for something they've forgotten.

'Ninety-nine... one hundred,' I say, banging my fist on the steering wheel. The sharp pain centres me, ensuring I stay focused.

I leave my car and walk casually up the road, appearing not to pay attention to anything going on around me. But inside, I'm buzzing with anticipation. Every sense is heightened. I notice everything: the chatter of birds in the trees, the distant hum of traffic and the thud of my shoes on the pavement.

At the house, I slip my key into the lock. The door opens with a soft click, and I step inside. The dog barks, but she's not going to do anything because she's in her crate. I'll go to see her. If she recognises me, she should quieten down.

I look around, hit by a wave of familiarity. I'm back. A shiver of pleasure runs down my spine. I walk into the kitchen. Everything's in its place. The woman's a total obsessive. Unlike me. I know how to live, how to be spontaneous. That's what Tom loves about me.

'Hello, Willow. It's only me,' I say, passing by the crate and going into the utility room to grab a few doggy treats. I slide them through the bars on the crate and she starts wolfing them down, her tail banging excitedly against the side. That should keep her quiet. Vivienne trusts her dog's judgement too much. If only she knew how easily animals can be won over with a few treats and a couple of gentle words.

I leave the kitchen and head upstairs, my footsteps light on the carpeted stairs. In Vivienne's bedroom, I open her wardrobe. My fingers run over the clothes. What did she wear for work today? I spot an empty hanger. Next to it, there's a navy silk blouse. I take it out and try it on. She's bigger than me, and it drowns my frame. So drab. Why does she wear this stuff? Is she trying to hide herself from people?

I take off the blouse and return it to the wardrobe. I'm about to close the door when I notice something's been shoved to the back. I reach in and pull out a carrier bag that wasn't there the last time I looked. Inside is a woman's T-shirt and several pairs of lacy underwear. They're all scrunched up. Why would she leave them in there and not put them away? That's weird. And totally different from how neat everything else is. I resist the urge to take them, to plant them somewhere compromising. Not yet. That's not part of today's plan.

I replace the bag and wander into the en-suite, opening drawers at random and rifling through their contents. What shall I do? My eyes land on her toothbrush standing in a glass. With a quick glance over my shoulder, I grab it and run it along the toilet rim. Then I put it back exactly where I found it. The thought of her using it later makes my skin tingle with satisfaction.

I head back downstairs and into the kitchen. Opening the cupboards, I see Tuesday's rainbow lunchbox. I put it in my bag with the intention of replacing it tomorrow morning, after they've left. That will cause grief for the little girl and – by default – Vivienne.

Now, what else can I do?

I remember the calendar she has on the wall and head over to it. How quaint that she uses such an old-fashioned way of remembering things. Each day is filled with neat handwriting, listing appointments, playdates and social events. So many opportunities to create chaos.

She has a dental appointment on Wednesday morning. Luckily, she's put the name of the dentist. I pull out my phone and call them.

'Good morning, Norwood Dental Surgery,' a woman says.

'Hi, this is Vivienne Campbell,' I reply in that congenial tone of hers. 'I've got an appointment on Wednesday at eleven-thirty, which I need to cancel because my daughter's not well. I'm so sorry for the short notice.' The lies roll off my tongue.

'That's fine,' the receptionist responds. 'Would you like to rearrange?'

'I'll give you a call,' I say, twirling a short strand of hair around my finger. 'I'm not sure at the moment.'

'I understand. Thanks for letting us know. I hope your daughter gets better soon.'

I end the call and put away my phone, a satisfied smirk playing on my lips. That'll be interesting for her. Maybe I should follow to see how it goes. Now what else shall I do...? I know...

I head into her study and pick up one of the framed photos on the bookcase. It's of Vivienne and her daughter. All smiling, so perfect. So fake. I slip it into my bag. Let's see if she notices.

I laugh to myself, the sound harsh and grating in the silent house. My whole body is humming with exhilaration. This is just the beginning. Each small act of disruption is a thread being pulled, slowly unravelling the fabric of her perfect life.

Before leaving, I take one last look around. Everything is as I found it, except for the small changes only I know about... for the moment. My fingers trail along the wall as I walk to the door, leaving invisible traces of my presence. I slip out of the house, locking the door behind me with practised care.

Walking back to my car, I allow myself a small smile. To anyone watching, I appear normal, going about my day. But inside, I'm revelling in the chaos that's about to be set in motion.

A neighbour hurries past with shopping bags, and I smile politely, playing my part perfectly.

I drive away, deliberating on what to do next. How else can I unsettle her? Make her question her sanity? The possibilities are endless, and I have all week to explore them. Each day will bring new opportunities to chip away at her certainty, her security... and her happiness.

My fingers tap an erratic rhythm on the steering wheel as I head home. Vivienne has no idea what's in store for her. But whatever it is, it serves her right. She deserves everything that's coming to her.

Once home, I sit on the sofa in the lounge with a mug of coffee, stroking my cat, Mink, who's lying beside me. A smile spreads across my face as I begin typing some notes into my phone. Ideas flow from my mind, each one more twisted than the last. I document everything meticulously: what I've done, what I plan to do, how she might react.

Control is everything.

NINE

VIVIENNE

Tuesday

'Don't cry, sweetheart,' I say to Lola when she starts wailing again after catching sight of the lunchbox she'd used today when I was popping it in the sink to wash.

Last night, when I went to get her lunch ready, I couldn't find the rainbow box.

I assumed that she'd left it at school last Thursday and we'd forgotten all about it, but I checked with the school earlier and discovered that it wasn't there. Lola's been upset on and off ever since.

'I want my lunchbox that Daddy gave me,' she says, her bottom lip jutting out in the way it often does before her emotions get the better of her and it turns into a full-blown temper tantrum.

'I'm sure we'll find it,' I say, trying to sound reassuring and crossing my fingers that it wasn't taken by someone at school, never to be seen again. 'You've still got the other one he got you. You can use it every day until we find the rainbow box.'

'But where is it?' Lola asks, continuing to sob.

I give a frustrated sigh. 'I don't know, love. I'll have another look, because it can't disappear into thin air, can it? We can always buy you another one if we can't find—'

'We can't,' Lola wails, sniffing loudly. 'Daddy told me it was special and there isn't another one like it. It came from Merica. Like my other one.' She starts crying again, her little body shaking with each sob.

'America, sweetheart,' I correct gently, though I know it's not the time for pronunciation lessons. 'And you're right. It is special.' I pause, remembering the way Lola's face would light up at the sight of the sparkly rainbow design. I should have been more careful keeping track of it.

I bend down to pick her up, giving her a little squeeze. 'It'll be fine. Don't worry,' I whisper, stroking her hair. 'Let's go into the lounge and I'll turn on the TV for you?'

'I don't want to,' she shouts loudly.

I pull my head back, her words ringing in my ears. 'Okay, you stay with me.' I try to let her go, but she clings on to me.

'Mummy,' Lola says, her voice softening as she wraps her little arms around my neck. 'Did you look under my bed? Sometimes things hide under there. Like Mr Whiskers.' She's referring to her stuffed cat that we'd spent three hours searching for last week, only to find it wedged between her bed and the wall.

'That's a good idea,' I say, touched by her attempt to help. 'Do you want to look, or shall we go together?'

She nods against my shoulder, her tears subsiding. 'And maybe in my school bag again? Sometimes things hide in the little pocket.'

I place her back on the floor. 'Okay, will you sit there then?' I point to one of the stools around the island. 'I'll wash the lunchbox you used today and put it away.'

'But Mummy,' she protests, 'I want to look under the bed now.'

'Just give me one minute, love. I need to get this done.' My head is starting to ache, the kind of dull throb that usually signals the start of a migraine.

Lola nods reluctantly and climbs onto the stool, leaving me to give the lunchbox a quick rinse and dry. I open the cupboard door to put it away, and there, right in front of my eyes, is the missing lunchbox.

What the...? How the hell did I miss it?

'It's here,' I exclaim, my voice sounding strange even to my own ears.

Lola clambers down and races over to the cupboard, staring in. Her face breaks into a huge smile. 'Thanks, Mummy,' she cries out, her earlier tears forgotten. She reaches for it, running her fingers over the glittery rainbow design. 'It's not lost anymore.'

'But how did it get there?' I ask, more to myself than my daughter. 'It definitely wasn't there yesterday.' I run my fingers along the shelf, as if touching it might help me understand how I could have possibly missed it. 'I looked in here three times and even took everything out to double-check.'

'Silly Mummy – you didn't see it when you looked,' Lola says, sounding more like Miles than ever. She hugs the lunchbox to her chest. 'Maybe it was playing hide-and-seek?'

I shake my head, still puzzled. 'It doesn't matter. It's here now.'

But it does matter. It matters because I'm certain it wasn't there yesterday. I'd emptied that entire cupboard, checking behind the other lunchboxes, the plastic containers, even the rarely used thermos flasks. 'Perhaps I looked in the wrong cupboard,' I say, trying to rationalise it, even though I know that's not true.

'Or maybe you had too much wine,' Lola pipes up innocently.

I freeze, looking down at her in shock. 'What?'

'When you looked,' Lola clarifies, still clutching her

precious lunchbox. 'I heard Daddy say that sometimes you drink too much wine. Is that why you couldn't see it, Mummy? Because the wine made your eyes fuzzy?'

Her words hit me like a physical blow. A surge of anger and hurt rushes through me. That's one hell of a loaded phrase for a five-year-old. I remember Miles saying it, but didn't realise it was in Lola's earshot. But what worries me more is the fact that I'm not entirely sure he's wrong. I'm certainly drinking more than I used to... But it's my relief from the stresses of looking after Lola and work, what with Miles not being here much.

'Well, it doesn't matter now because the lunchbox is here,' I say, trying to keep my voice light. 'I take it you'd now like to watch some cartoons?' I force a smile.

'Yes, please,' Lola says eagerly. 'Can I take my lunchbox with me? I don't want it to get lost again.'

'Of course, sweetheart.'

We head into the lounge, and I turn on the television.

Once Lola's settled, I retreat to my study, needing some time alone to think things through. Sitting in my chair, I swivel around, staring at my surroundings. My eyes focus on the bookcase and the array of photos on top. Where's the one of me with Lola when we went to the New Forest? It was in a gilt frame that Miles bought for me.

I start at one end of the bookcase and stare at each photo in turn, to make sure I haven't missed it, but it's not there. Maybe Miles took it with him? But if he did, why didn't he tell me? Unless he forgot. Or maybe I was the one to move it somewhere else and forgot. That seems to be par for the course now.

Anyway, I'm not going to worry about it. There are more pressing matters to deal with. Like Miles talking about my drinking when Lola can hear. I'm certain he only has my best interests at heart – that's one of the reasons I love him so much – but even so, it's important that he keep his comments to a time when Lola's asleep or not around. Not that my drinking should concern him. I'm a social drinker, that's all. A couple of glasses of wine with dinner isn't a crime, is it? Even if it is increasingly *every* evening...

I lean back in my chair, closing my eyes for a moment. The house is quiet except for the faint sound of cartoons coming from the lounge. I should be relieved that we found Lola's lunchbox, but instead, I feel unsettled.

Maybe I am drinking too much if I can't remember where I put things or if I'm looking for photos that aren't there. Or maybe it's stress. Being a working mother isn't easy. Although I've done it for five years, so it's not exactly new to me. Maybe it's because I keep feeling like something isn't right. I need to snap out of it, because thinking like that will attract bad things. I've read all about the law of attraction – from now on, I'll stop looking for inconsistencies in my life.

I open my eyes and glance at the clock. It's time to make Lola's supper. Standing up, I catch a glimpse of myself in the mirror hanging on the wall. For a second, I don't recognise the weary-looking woman staring back at me.

I blink, and the moment passes. It's just me, Vivienne. A normal mum trying to hold it all together. Juggling home, work and at times, feeling like a single parent. I straighten my shoulders and head back to the lounge to check on Lola.

'One day at a time,' I tell myself. That's all I can do.

TEN

VIVIENNE

Wednesday

After driving round for ages, I finally find a parking spot down
one of the side streets in the Fulflood area of Winchester and
then make a mad dash to the dentist for my appointment. I'd
intended to work from home today, but at the last minute, an
urgent meeting had been called at work, and I'd been ordered to
attend. There'd been a client complaint against one of my team
and the HR director wanted me and the staff member to see
him to discuss it. I debated saying no and asking for the time of
the meeting to be changed, but knowing what a tyrant the
director could be, I agreed, thinking that I'd still have time to get
to my appointment on time. Of course – typical of my luck – it
had overrun. I'm only five minutes late, so hopefully they won't
mind.

The dental surgery is in a parade of shops, sandwiched
between a hairdresser's and a small café, close to the city centre.
On arriving, I push open the door and rush to the reception.

'So sorry I'm late,' I gasp at the woman behind the desk,

breathing heavily from my dash from the car. 'My appointment's at eleven-thirty with Heather. It's Vivienne Campbell.'

The receptionist glances up from the computer on her desk with a puzzled expression on her face. 'I'm sorry, Mrs Campbell, but I haven't got you in with Heather today.'

I blink, confusion setting in. 'What do you mean? My appointment's today at eleven-thirty. I know I'm a few minutes late, but I was definitely booked in for today.'

I open my bag, pull out my phone, and bring up the calendar. 'Look, here it is.' I hold out my phone and point at the entry.

The receptionist glances at my phone, then looks back at her computer screen, pressing the mouse several times. 'Yes, I can see you *had* an appointment at the time you said, but according to the records, it was cancelled the day before yesterday. You spoke to our other receptionist, who was on duty then. Monday's my day off.'

I shake my head, feeling increasingly bewildered. 'That's ridiculous. Why would I cancel it? It's for my six-monthly check-up and I really need to speak to Heather about a problem I'm having when eating hot or very cold food. All I can think is that your other receptionist cancelled my appointment by mistake.'

The receptionist gives me an apologetic look. 'If that's the case, I don't know how it happened.'

I take a deep breath. I don't want to have a go at the woman because I hate confrontation and it's not her fault, but this is absurd. 'I think someone else cancelled their appointment with Heather and somehow mine was cancelled instead.'

'Well... I suppose that might have happened,' the receptionist says, looking uncertain. 'But I'm not sure how, because the computer program doesn't allow for errors like that. But in this instance...' Her voice falls away.

'Can you fit me in now?' I ask, hoping that this can quickly be sorted out.

The receptionist shakes her head. 'I'm sorry, that's not possible. Once your appointment became free, it was offered to someone on our waiting list.'

I run a hand through my hair, feeling completely lost. 'So, what am I meant to do? I've literally driven from work in Southampton just for this appointment.'

'I'm really sorry, Mrs Campbell. All I can do is apologise again and book you another appointment for your check-up.'

I sigh heavily, my shoulders slumping. 'Okay, I'll take the next one you have available, please.'

The woman stares at the screen. 'I can do two weeks today at the same time. Does that work for you?'

'Yes, that's fine, thanks. I'll take that,' I mutter, feeling defeated.

Visiting the dentist has never been a favourite occupation of mine, and days ago, I began steeling myself for what was to come. At my age, I should be better, but my parents took me to a dentist who refused to give children sedation for fillings when I was a kid. It scarred me for life.

I leave the building and return to my car. Shall I go back to Southampton or work from home? I have loads on, but I can easily do it from the house before collecting Lola from school.

Home it is.

Before starting the engine, I mull over all the bizarre things that have been happening to me this week. The lunchbox. The missing photo, and now this. I'm almost certain that I didn't cancel my dentist appointment, so they must have made a mistake. But why am I feeling unsure...? Why do I feel like I'm beginning to lose the plot?

Maybe I'll call Miles and tell him what's happened.

Except he most likely won't be able to answer his phone, and even if he can, he'll probably say I cancelled it and then forgot. Which is the logical answer. But I didn't. I know I didn't. I'd have remembered... Wouldn't I?

Suddenly, I'm not sure *what* I remember anymore. Maybe something came up at work and I hurriedly cancelled my appointment, then totally forgot about it? Yes... that must have been what happened. I shake my head, trying to clear the fog that seems to be settling over my thoughts, and give a loud sigh.

I pull out of my parking space and head in the direction of home. But throughout the journey, I find myself second-guessing every turn and every traffic light. Do I always take this route home? Has that shop always been there? I grip the steering wheel tighter, to reassure myself that it's all okay and I'm imagining all this disruption.

When I finally pull into our driveway, I sit in the car for a moment to collect myself. My house looks the same as always, but for a split second, I wonder if I've come to the right place.

This is ridiculous. Of course it's my house.

After getting out of the car and opening the front door, I walk inside, my footsteps echoing in the empty hallway. The house feels different somehow, but I can't put my finger on why. I wander from room to room, touching familiar objects, trying to ground myself.

In the kitchen, I pour myself a glass of water, my hand shaking slightly.

What's happening to me? Am I losing my mind? It's like my reality is shifting, and I can't keep up.

Suddenly it hits me, right between the eyes.

What if I've got early-onset dementia? It might be rare, but it *can* happen to someone of my age. I remember watching a documentary on it and being scared that something like that could happen me. Could I have attracted it to myself?

Whoa, Vivienne. It's a big step to go from a few weird things happening to having dementia.

So what if I've forgotten a few things and not seen things

that are there? And even if I did cancel my dentist appointment without remembering having done so, that doesn't mean anything. I've been through a lot worse in my life and come through it.

I need to take a breath and pull myself together. I'm *not* going crazy. I'm almost sure of it.

ELEVEN

AMELIA

Thursday

I sit in my car waiting for Vivienne to arrive home. My eyes dart back and forth, scanning the street while my heart pounds with anticipation. My cheek twitches and I give it a rough rub before focusing on what I'm here to do. The familiar surge of adrenaline courses through my veins. Today, everything changes.

I'm stepping it up.

If Vivienne follows her usual routine, she'll arrive home shortly with the child and immediately take Willow for a walk. Lucky for me, she's a creature of habit, so I don't expect her to do anything different today. The weather's fine, so there's no reason for her to change her plans. But this time, I won't just be watching. Today, we'll be meeting face to face. The thought sends a delicious shiver down my spine.

I've already been into her house again today. I emptied the dishwasher, putting things away in the wrong place, and pulled the TV plug out of the socket in the lounge. I also moved around the coats hanging on the hooks in the entrance porch—

My thoughts are cut short as I spot her car driving down the road and turning into the drive. Right on schedule. They head into the house. Vivienne's shoulders are noticeably tense. Am I getting to her already?

My fingers tap an irregular rhythm on the steering wheel as I count the minutes until she reappears.

After ten, they emerge. Willow trots happily beside them, the lead in Vivienne's hand. She's wearing her usual walking outfit – those ridiculous jazzy leggings and an oversized fleece that makes her look like she's trying too hard to be casual.

I snuggle down in the seat until they pass and then get out of the car, my movements deliberate and controlled. Keeping my distance, I follow. My hands are in the pockets of my hoodie and my head is down, in case they turn around; I'm not yet ready to be seen.

They enter the park. It's quiet. Secluded. The late-afternoon sun casts long shadows across the path, and a cool breeze rustles through the trees. Perfect conditions for our 'chance' encounter.

My heart races with excitement rather than nerves. It's time to make my move.

I quicken my pace, rounding the path until I'm in front of them. Vivienne stops abruptly, her eyes slowly widening as recognition dawns. I notice how, for some reason, she instinctively pulls her daughter closer. Surely she can't believe I'm a threat? Well, she's right.

'Vivienne, is that you?' I ask, bringing my hand to my mouth and feigning surprise. I've practised this moment in front of my mirror countless times.

'Amelia?' Vivienne's voice wavers, and I savour the uncertainty in her tone.

'Yes, it's me.' I smile, closing the distance between us. My left eye twitches, but I ignore it, focusing instead on maintaining the perfect balance of friendly and hesitant in my expression. 'I'm off work this week and it is such a nice day, so I came for a walk in the park. I wanted to clear my head, to be honest.' The lies flow smoothly, each word carefully chosen to seem casual yet hint at vulnerability. 'I noticed you all from over there, but wasn't totally sure it actually was you, which is why I came over. Several times I thought about phoning you to say sorry for not being there when you got home after I housesat. But then I thought you might be mad with me and so backed out. Which is stupid, I know.' I glance down at the ground, acting as if I'm ashamed by my actions.

'I must admit to being surprised that you'd gone but we were late and I hadn't called,' Vivienne replied with a shrug.

'Well I'm really sorry,' I repeat. 'How have you been?'

I watch her throat move as she swallows, noting how her free hand moves to touch her collar nervously. Her eyes are wary. She's definitely unsettled.

My plan's already working even better than I'd hoped.

'I've been okay,' Vivienne says, sounding strained. She shifts her weight from one foot to the other, and I mirror her body language subtly, like they say in those better-communication books, to create a connection between us. 'It's just... I don't know. Things are busy at work and home. Sometimes, it's hard to... to deal with everything.'

I nod, ensuring my expression is sympathetic while inwardly rejoicing at how easily she's opening up. 'I totally get it. I've had a tough time of it recently, too.' I pause, letting my words sink in so she thinks that we're both in the same boat. After a few seconds, I break the silence, leaning in slightly. 'Listen, if you ever need to talk, I'm here.' I rest my hand gently on her arm, noting how she tenses but doesn't pull away. 'I know we hardly know each other, but sometimes it's easier to talk to someone who's not so close.'

'Thanks, Amelia,' Vivienne says softly. 'That really means a lot.'

If it wasn't for the fact I know what she's really like, I'd be fooled by the look of gratitude that flashes across the woman's face. But the butter-wouldn't-melt expression doesn't wash with me. I have no sympathy for her.

'Look, you've got my number if you need it.' I give her arm a gentle squeeze before letting go, already imagining how this connection will allow me to weave myself into her life, strand by poisonous strand.

Then I turn my attention to the little girl who's been playing with Willow. What was her name again? I wrack my brain for a moment, refusing to let this small detail derail my performance.

'How have you been... Lola?' I say, the name coming to me just in time. I bend down slightly, making sure to keep my movements gentle and unthreatening.

The child turns around and looks at me, her big, blue eyes curious. 'I'm very well, thank you,' she says politely. Then, as if a dam has burst, words pour out of her. 'And guess what? We found my lunchbox. It went missing and we found it and it's my favourite one that Daddy bought for me all the way from Merica.'

The child's voice grates on my nerves like nails on a chalkboard.

I glance back at Vivienne, who's shaking her head, a genuine smile softening her features for the first time during our encounter. 'She means *America*. It happened a few days ago, but she's still talking about it.'

'I remember your lunchboxes. You showed them to me.' I force a smile, though my cheek twitches again. 'Thank goodness you found them.' I turn back to Vivienne, not waiting for the child to reply. 'I won't bother you any longer.' No need to risk overdoing it. 'Text if you'd like to grab a coffee sometime and have a chat.'

Vivienne nods, a tight smile on her face. 'Thanks. It's very kind of you to offer.'

I give them both a final smile and bend down to pat the dog, using the moment to observe how Vivienne's posture has changed. She still seems uncertain, but there's a hint of relief in her eyes. As I straighten up, I catch her eye, and she gives an appreciative smile.

So easy. So pathetically easy.

I walk away, allowing myself a tiny smirk. The foundation has been laid. Vivienne's defences are weakening. Soon, very soon, I'll be able to—

One step at a time. One step at a time. I need to be patient and not rush anything.

Stopping behind a tree, I watch Vivienne, the child and the dog continue their walk, their figures growing smaller in the distance. Vivienne's shoulders are still hunched and her stride quick. I'd love to know what's going through her mind. Is she pleased to have met me again? Does she think she's found a kindred spirit? I hope so.

I go back to the car, but don't drive off immediately. Instead, I sit here, replaying every moment of our interaction. My performance was flawless, if I do say so myself. The right mix of friendly and hesitant, concerned yet casual.

Laughter erupts from me – sharp and sudden, and my cheek twitches violently. I press my hand against it. I'm too happy and excited to be bothered. Everything's falling into place.

With one last look at her house, I pull away from the kerb. The real game is yet to come. And I can't wait to play. After all, I've been practising for this moment for longer than Vivienne could possibly imagine. Ever since I learnt about what she'd done. Her days of peaceful dog walks and lost lunchboxes are numbered.

TWELVE
VIVIENNE

Monday

This weird feeling that something's off is with me all the time. I pace around the kitchen, my fingers tracing the edge of the worktop as if searching for evidence of an intruder. Nothing seems right. I forget that I've done things – like when I went to empty the dishwasher the other day and found it empty. And then I couldn't get the TV to work; turns out, it was unplugged from the wall. I never do that, and when I asked Lola if she'd done it, she said she hadn't. Also, things seem to randomly *move* from their usual spot to somewhere else. It's just plain weird.

It was nice bumping into Amelia last week and I appreciated her offer to listen. I've thought about her a lot over the weekend, and several times was tempted to take her up on it because she's right; it might help to have a chat with someone I don't know well. Someone who has no vested interest in me, my family or my work.

I stop pacing and lean against the fridge, letting out a long breath. I'll do it.

Picking up my phone, I send her a text:

> Thanks for the offer to talk. I'd really like to take you up on it. Are you around on Saturday? I'm going into town for a few bits, and we can meet in one of the cafés near the cathedral.

Just sending the message makes me feel better.

I head into the lounge to check on Lola, who's in front of the television watching a children's nature programme. I feel guilty about the amount of screen time she has these days. You read that it can be detrimental to her development, but it doesn't seem to be harming her. Her small form is silhouetted against the flickering screen and she's clutching her favourite doll tightly to her chest.

We haven't had anything to eat yet because we're waiting for Miles to arrive home. He phoned out of the blue last night and said he'd be coming home today for a couple of days. When he asked if everything was okay, I pretended it was so as not to worry him. It will be easier to tell him when we're together. I glance at my watch, willing the hands to move faster.

Suddenly, I hear the door opening. My heart leaps, and I rush to the hall, a smile breaking across my face. Now Miles is here, everything feels okay.

'You're early,' I say, drinking in his presence – those piercing dark eyes and striking features. Even after all our time together, just seeing him standing there steals my breath away, like the very first time our eyes met.

'Yes, we got back in record time.' He grins. 'The wind must have been with us.'

I raise an eyebrow. 'What? Seriously? The wind makes you go quicker when you're flying?'

'Not exactly, but wind can make a flight longer or shorter depending on the type it is.' He laughs and reaches out to pull me into a long hug. I melt into his arms. 'Actually, I left earlier than originally planned.'

'Daddyyyy,' Lola shouts, careering out of the lounge and rushing over. She wraps herself around his legs.

Miles looks at me over the top of Lola's head, concern etching his features. 'Are you okay?' he mouths.

I shake my head slightly, and his brow furrows.

'Right, young lady,' Miles says, gently disentangling himself from Lola's grip. 'You get back to the television because I'm going to help Mummy in the kitchen. I'll be in to see you shortly – I hope it's all tidy in there.'

Another of the things I love about Miles is that he's as tidy as I am. Probably tidier. He always hangs up his clothes and puts everything away. I couldn't stand it if he was any other way.

'Of course it is, Daddy,' Lola says, skipping into the lounge to her spot in front of the TV, doll in tow.

I retreat to the kitchen, Miles following close behind. He then turns to me and takes both of my hands in his.

'What's the matter?' he asks, his voice low and gentle, concern shining from his eyes.

I take a deep breath, deciding to tell him everything. 'You're going to think this is ridiculous, but I'm feeling off all the time. Lola's lunchbox went missing, and then it was there. I'm sure there was a photo on the bookcase in a particular frame that's not there anymore. My dentist appointment was mysteriously cancelled. The dishwasher unloaded itself... Nothing's quite right.'

'Are you sure?' Miles asks, his thumbs rubbing soothing circles on the backs of my hands. 'You've got quite a lot going on – you're probably doing stuff on autopilot and not registering.'

I pull my hands away, running them through my hair in frustration. 'I don't know. Maybe. I'm questioning everything I do now.'

Miles steps closer, placing his hands on my shoulders. He locks eyes with mine. 'Look, I think you're just stressed. You've been working too hard, looking after Lola while I'm away. Why don't we go away on Saturday? I'm meant to be on standby and was going to stay at one of the army bases for the night in case of an early start, but I'll book the time off and come home instead. I'll get someone else to cover me for the night, but will have to go back to work on Sunday when we get home. I'll be back by lunchtime and we can all go to Lymington and stay somewhere overlooking the ocean? Lola and Willow will enjoy it too. I'll take care of them both and you can relax.'

I nod slowly. 'It's tempting. But I'm really busy at work and might not have time to get everything ready.'

'You won't need much – it's only for one night.'

Miles caresses my face with his fingers, and I feel myself relaxing. Until I suddenly remember something and jump back.

'Oh no, I've just sent a text to Amelia to see if she wants to go out for coffee on Saturday.'

'Amelia?' Miles asks with a frown.

'The housesitter I used a few weeks ago.'

'Well, cancel it,' Miles says with a shrug. 'I'm sure she'll understand.'

'She hasn't answered yet, but I'll send another text...' I trail off, suddenly aware of how odd it might seem to Amelia that first I arrange something and then want to cancel.

'How come you want to see her?' Miles asks.

'We bumped into each other in the park and she looked as harried as I was feeling,' I explain. 'She suggested that we meet up for a chat sometime if I wanted to. It was very kind of her. She's really nice. I can see us becoming friends, which sounds ridiculous, as we've only just met. It's nice to have someone who lives close by. That's the trouble with working in Southampton – none of my colleagues live around here.'

Miles nods, but there's a flicker of concern in his eyes. 'I can't wait to meet her,' he says, smiling and pulling me into his arms.

'I wish you were here all the time,' I murmur against his chest.

I know we've only been together for three and a half years, but it feels like forever. I can still feel the ping in my stomach the day I first bumped into him – literally – in the supermarket car park and ended up dropping my shopping. He was kind and charming and even helped me pick everything up.

He insisted on carrying the bags to my car and loading them into the boot. We were married within six months and from that day, Lola has called him Daddy. We didn't even ask her to; she did it of her own accord. It was so nice to finally have someone to confide in. Although he doesn't know everything... I learnt my lesson the hard way on that front, after telling a previous partner my full history. I won't make that mistake again. And Miles not knowing doesn't matter, because it all happened a long time ago and doesn't affect our lives.

Even if it does still haunt my dreams from time to time.

'It will all be worth it when I finally retire,' he reassures me. 'Fifteen more years and then I'm done. We've talked about this. The years will fly by, trust me.' He releases my hands and then goes to the cupboard and takes out a glass.

I lean against the counter, watching him fill it with water. My stomach churns with an uncomfortable mixture of hope and doubt. 'That's such a long time,' I say quietly. 'Fifteen years of you being away so much... Lola will be grown up by then.'

He takes a long drink before answering. 'Let's not get into all that right now. Tell me more about Amelia. What made you click with her so quickly?'

'Oh, I don't know... She just seems genuine. Down to earth. When we were talking, it felt...' I pause, trying to find the right words. 'It felt like she really understood what I was saying about feeling off-kilter lately.'

Miles sets his glass down with a sharp click. 'Do you think I don't understand?'

'Of course not. That's not what I meant,' I say quickly. 'It's just that sometimes it helps to talk to someone outside of everything. Someone who doesn't have to worry about me.'

He runs a hand through his hair, a gesture I know means he's frustrated. 'I worry because I care, Vivienne. And honestly, I'm a bit concerned that you're confiding in someone you barely know when you've got me right here.'

The words sting more than they should. 'It's not about confiding, it's about friendship. Being a pilot's wife can be lonely sometimes, and you're the one who's always saying I should make more local friends.'

'Yes, but—' He's cut off by the sound of Lola calling from the living room.

'Daddy. Mummy. Come look at this.'

Miles and I exchange a look, and I can see him consciously softening his expression. 'We'll talk more later,' he says, touching my arm briefly as he passes.

I follow him to the living room, trying to smooth my features into something more neutral before Lola sees me, but the nagging feeling in my gut only intensifies.

He's my husband, so surely he should understand why I want to be friends with someone who lives close by? Maybe he doesn't want me to confide in someone he doesn't know. I don't know why though – she's hardly a threat. And it's not like I know anything about his missions to divulge them to anyone. I'll introduce them to each other and he'll see Amelia's as nice as I've said.

THIRTEEN

AMELIA

Saturday

I slip the key into the lock. My heart isn't just pounding now – it's singing. Each beat drives me forwards with a purpose that makes my skin tingle. The soft click as the key turns sends a delicious shiver down my spine.

That perfect husband, whisking Vivienne away for the weekend – he might as well have gift-wrapped this opportunity. I ease the door open.

The darkness inside the house wraps around me and I stand still, letting my eyes adjust, breathing in Vivienne's lingering perfume. Vanilla and jasmine. I curl my lip in disgust, but take another deep breath anyway. I want to remember this moment.

The beam of my torch catches the mirror on the wall, and I reach out to touch the glass, leaving a single fingerprint in the middle. Will she notice? Will she clean it obsessively, like she does everything else?

A floorboard creaks upstairs and I freeze, my muscles coiling tight. My breath catches in my throat as I listen, with my head tilted to one side. Nothing follows, but my heart is hammering loudly.

It was just the house settling.

I know they're away, but for some reason, I still creep up the stairs, placing each foot with careful precision. My body buzzes with electricity, every nerve ending alive and firing. At the top, I pause, letting my torch beam swing lazily around the landing.

I head for her bedroom and wander over to her dressing table, where I deliberately disturb the precise arrangement of perfume bottles. I then go to her wardrobe, running my hands over her carefully organised clothes. I pull out a white silky blouse with fine cream stripes and tug at the bottom until the fabric strains and rips.

'Oops,' I mumble, hanging it back carefully. Will she notice right away? Or will it be just before an important meeting when she finds the hole?

Next stop: the bed. This was the main reason for me to be here.

I run my tongue over my lips, tasting salt. I've been sweating, I realise, but it's not from fear. It's excitement. Pure, undiluted excitement coursing through my veins like a drug.

I open the bag I'm carrying and pull out the new sheets bought especially for this occasion. I'd taken a photo of hers earlier in the week and researched online until I found the same design, with an embossed lily, only in a shade darker. I strip the bed, my movements quick and precise, and then replace the old sheets with the new ones. I smooth them into place, humming softly under my breath.

If this doesn't cause Vivienne to think she's lost her mind, then nothing will.

Will she notice immediately that they're not her original sheets? Or will it dawn on her gradually? Oh, to be a fly on the wall when she does discover it – however long it takes.

Suddenly, a shrill ring pierces the silence. I gasp, my whole body jerking as if electrified. My heart leaps into my throat as I whirl around, the torch beam dancing wildly across the walls. There, on the nightstand, a phone glows in the darkness like an accusing eye.

Who even has a landline these days?

I suck in several long breaths, willing my racing heart to slow.

The ringing continues until there's a beep, and a voice fills the room, making me flinch. 'Hey, Viv, it's Sarah from work. Sorry to call at the weekend. I wanted to chat about the agenda for next week's meeting. Give me a call when you can. Bye.'

I let out a shaky breath, relief making my knees weak. Just her work colleague. Not someone checking on the house. Not the police. But my skin is crawling now; every shadow seems to hide a threat.

I need to get it together. It's not like anyone knows I'm here.

I head downstairs to the kitchen, moving with purpose. I shift a saucepan two inches to the left. Turn mugs so their handles face the wrong way. Rearrange coffee pods so the flavours are all mixed up. I remove a china mug from the dishwasher and pop it into my bag. Each small change is a brushstroke in my masterpiece of confusion.

As I work, scenarios play through my mind like a favourite movie. Vivienne reaching for her morning coffee, finding everything slightly wrong. The growing confusion in her eyes. The way she'll question herself, then her family. The moment when she realises something is very, very wrong, but can't prove it. Can't explain it. Can't escape it.

Next, I go through to the lounge and have fun making minute changes to the cushions and ornaments. After that, I make one final sweep of the house, checking my handiwork. It's an art form, really. Too much, and she'll know someone was here. Too little, and she might not notice at all. But this is perfect. Like a spider's web: invisible until you're already caught in it.

The front door closes behind me with a soft click, and a wave of euphoria so intense washes over me that I have to lean against the wall for a moment.

Sweet dreams, Vivienne. While you still can.

I hurry down the driveway towards where I've parked the car, my footsteps seeming too loud in the quiet street. Each house I pass is dark and silent, their windows like blank eyes, unseeing. They have no idea what just transpired. What's still to come.

Behind the wheel of my car, a laugh bubbles up from deep inside me. It sounds slightly maniacal even to my own ears, but I don't care. I let it out, and it fills the car with its wild energy.

The streetlights blur as I drive, my mind already racing ahead to the next phase of my plan. My fingers flex on the steering wheel, remembering the little touches of chaos I've left behind, lying in wait like land mines in her perfect world. Soon they'll start to detonate, one by one.

I'd love to witness Vivienne's face when they do. The confusion, the doubt, the fear. It's almost enough to make me turn around to hide and watch it unfold. But I won't. For this payoff, patience is key.

FOURTEEN

VIVIENNE

Sunday

'Thanks so much for such an amazing time,' I say to Miles with a smile, and reaching my hand on his arm as he pulls into the drive and parks close to the front door. 'It's been ages since I've felt so relaxed and ready to face everything that comes my way.'

And I mean it. Being away from home made me rationalise my life and realise that I've been so wound up that it coloured my judgement.

'Anything for you,' he says, winking. 'Let's get everything unloaded because I've got to head off.'

My stomach drops. Even though I knew he would have to leave for work straight away, now the time is here, my newfound confidence is wavering. 'I don't suppose there's any chance of you coming back home if you don't end up flying?' I ask, trying not to sound like I'm pleading. But it would finish the weekend off so nicely if he was with me until Monday.

'You don't know how much I wish that were possible,' he says with a loud sigh. 'But I'm fairly certain I'll be flying because one of the other pilots' partner has COVID, and so he can't go up.'

I exhale, briefly wishing that *we* all had COVID to prevent him from leaving, and then mentally retracting the thought because I wouldn't want to wish that on anyone, especially Lola.

'Never mind,' I say, trying to hide my disappointment. I don't want him leaving thinking I'm all upset because he'll only worry.

'Come on, let's get you girls out of here,' Miles says with a smile.

He carries Lola, who's fallen asleep in her travel seat, up to her bedroom, laying her on the bed. Then we go back outside to bring in the cases. Despite what Miles had said when suggesting the trip, of course I'd overpacked.

'Do you have time for a coffee?' I ask, wanting to prolong the moment before he leaves.

'No, sorry, I've really got to dash. You know what the traffic's like on a Sunday evening with everyone heading home, and add to that the roadworks that for some reason seem to be popping up everywhere I drive. I can't be late. Come and give me a kiss goodbye.'

He takes my hand and draws me close with tender urgency. I melt into his embrace, winding my arms around his neck as if they were always meant to be there. Our lips meet and it's like there's only this moment, only us, wrapped in a kiss that speaks of longing and promise. Minutes pass like heartbeats until he slowly pulls away. A soft groan of protest escapes my lips, already missing his warmth.

'You better go,' I whisper, managing a brave smile despite the ache in my chest. 'Fly safe.'

I walk him to the front door and wave goodbye. After his car is out of sight, I head to Lola's room to undress her. She'll have to do without cleaning her teeth – it won't matter for one night. She barely moves, which is hardly surprising given the way she was charging around all over the place while we were away.

I head downstairs to the kitchen to put on the kettle and make myself a hot drink. As much as I'd love a coffee, it really is too late, or I'll be wide awake all night. Opening the cupboard where the mugs are kept, I do a double take. Everything looks slightly different. It certainly wasn't like that when I left, I'm sure... I think.

Where's my favourite mug?

It's one Miles gave me for my last birthday and I use it all the time. I check the dishwasher but's not in there. I look again in the cupboard but still can't see it.

This is really weird.

I take out another mug, make myself some hot chocolate and head for the lounge. I perch on the edge of the leather sofa, looking around, frowning. Why are the cushions like that? They should be indented in the middle and upright against the back, but now they're placed in the corners of the chairs and sofa.

Maybe Miles changed them? Yes, that's it. Or even Lola. She does like messing with the cushions.

I look around the room again. 'Hang on a minute,' I say aloud, my eyes narrowing. 'Why is the green glass bird ornament on the left side of the television, when it's always on the right?' I place my mug on the table beside me and rest my head in my hands.

What's going on? I was feeling fine after our weekend together. But now this weird feeling has returned and I'm reeling.

A terrible thought strikes me. What if I've been moving these things myself and have totally forgotten? My breath comes in short gasps. What if it really is early-onset dementia? No, it can't be. I'm way too young. Seriously, way too young.

Except... It can happen early. I know that for a fact. It might be rare, but even at my age, thirty-eight, it's possible.

What would Lola do if that happened? What would Miles—?

No, I'm not even going to think about this. I'm fine. I know it. Miles wouldn't leave me alone with Lola if he thought there was anything wrong with me. But would he notice? It's not like he spends a lot of time with us.

I finish my chocolate, put the mug into the dishwasher and take a glass of water upstairs to bed. In the bathroom, I brush my teeth, my movements frantic and uncoordinated. Then I pick up the book beside the bed and pull back the sheets.

I freeze, staring directly at them. 'These aren't my sheets,' I whisper.

Mine are white, and these are cream.

I sit heavily on the bed, my mind whirling. Did I wash the white sheets and they've lost their colour? Or have I bought a new set and forgotten?

'Did. I. Buy. New. Sheets?' I demand, my voice echoing in the quiet room and verging on sounding hysterical.

I clench my fists and bang them on the bed. What the hell's going on? Why am I doing these things?

I curl up on the bed, hugging my knees to my chest. The room seems to spin around me as doubts and fears crowd my mind. Did I really have such a perfect weekend with Miles, or am I imagining that too? Is Lola really asleep in her room, or did I dream that?

I stumble out of bed and rush to Lola's room, needing to check on her. She's there, sleeping peacefully. I let out a shaky breath and lean against the doorframe, my legs weak with relief.

Back in my room, I try to calm myself by taking deep breaths. Nothing's wrong, I tell myself. I'm just tired, that's all. But as I lie in bed, staring at the ceiling, sleep eludes me. Every creak of the house makes me jump. Is someone here? Did I lock the door? I get up twice to check, finding it securely locked both times.

I toss and turn, my mind replaying the events of the day. Was Miles as affectionate as I remember, or am I reading too much into his actions, too? Why did he seem so eager to leave? Surely he could've stayed a little longer after I asked him.

My thoughts become more frantic and I begin imagining worst-case scenarios: Miles never coming back; Lola being taken away by social services because I'm losing my mind and ending up alone and confused in a care home; Miles and Lola having me admitted to a mental-health institution that I'm not allowed to leave…

Stop it.

I'm blowing this up out of proportion. Everything's fine.

But despite these thoughts, I know that it isn't. My mind's playing tricks on me and I'm seriously losing the plot. That's the top and bottom of it. It's like I now have no control over anything in my life.

I sit up in bed, hugging my knees to my chest, rocking gently forwards and backwards. The shadows in the room seem to stretch and distort, taking on menacing shapes. I shudder, then close my eyes tightly, trying to shut out the world around me.

'I am not crazy,' I whisper to myself. 'I am not crazy. I am not crazy.'

But even as I say the words, a part of me wonders if they're even true. How can I trust my own perception of events when everything feels so off-kilter? The mug, the cushions, the sheets, the dentist, lunchbox, the photo… Small things, but they add up to an extremely disconcerting whole.

I reach for my phone, desperate to connect with someone – anyone – who might help me down off this ledge. But who can I call at this hour? Who'd understand? I stare at the screen, my finger hovering over Miles's name.

But what would I say to him?

Hello, darling. You're not going to believe this, but I think I'm losing my mind over rearranged cushions and the sheets in our bedroom changing colour?

No, I can't call him. He'd only worry, and that might affect his ability to fly safely.

I put the phone down, feeling more alone than ever. The silence of the house presses in on me, broken only by the sound of my ragged breathing.

'Get it together, Vivienne,' I mutter. 'You're just overtired. Everything will be fine in the morning. Try to sleep. Count sheep or something.'

And that's another thing – I seem to be talking out loud to myself more and more these days. Is that yet another sign of something being wrong with me?

But as I lie back down, pulling the unfamiliar fresh-smelling cream sheets up to my chin, all I can think of is that something fundamental has shifted in my life. It's as if I've stepped into a parallel universe where everything is just a little bit wrong. Maybe I'm having a psychotic experience? When everything is real, but it's not... but... I don't think that could be right. I haven't lost contact with reality. Definitely not. Have I?

Suddenly, a thought enters my head and I sit up, my eyes wide.

Amelia.

Of course, why didn't I think of that sooner? I'll talk to her. She'll be able to give me a logical explanation for all this. I'm sure of it.

Sighing loudly, I pick up my phone from the side and hurriedly send Amelia a text, asking to rearrange our cancelled coffee because I could do with someone to talk to. Once I hit send, I replace the phone and then close my eyes, willing sleep to come. But in the darkness, questions continue to swirl with no let-up.

Am I losing my grip on reality?

Or is there something more going on... something I can't quite grasp right now, but that once I know will put an end to all this?

Exhaustion finally begins to overtake me and between yawns, one last thought floats through my mind, and it's a doozy: if I can't trust my own perceptions, what can I trust?

FIFTEEN

AMELIA

'You're looking very pleased with yourself,' Tom says as he comes in with a tray of cheese and crackers for us both, which he sets down on the coffee table. The aroma of aged cheddar fills the air: a familiar comfort that feels oddly out of place with the excitement bubbling inside me.

I look up at him, unable to contain my smile. The corners of my mouth twitch, threatening to burst into a full-fledged grin. 'Well, I suppose I am,' I reply, a rush of excitement coursing through me. 'I've had the perfect week off.'

Tom sits next to me on the sofa and helps himself to several crackers – crumbs falling onto his lap, which he brushes onto the floor – and tops them with some cheese. I refrain from moaning at him for being messy because I don't want to spoil the moment. It won't take long to vacuum it up later.

I totally love Tom, but he's so untidy that it drives me crazy sometimes. Our home is so different to Vivienne's, it's not even funny. Then again, who wants to live in a show home? Hardly daring to breathe all the time.

'I wish I could've spent more time with you, but this project is threatening to overrun and I have to be on it.'

'That's okay. If you don't do a good job, people won't want to employ you.'

Tom's a project management consultant and constantly in demand. We only moved to Winchester from Manchester because he had so much work down here and he was fed up with all the travel. It wasn't an easy decision, because property prices are so much higher here and it means we have a bigger mortgage. But that aside, I was happy to move and have him around more. I was quite lonely when we were living up north.

My mind flashes back to when we first met. I knew immediately after swiping right that we were meant for each other. And after meeting for coffee the first time – when we chatted all afternoon and into the evening – I was totally smitten. We've been together ever since.

'True,' he agrees with a smile.

I glance at his face. There's something about the way he's looking at me, with such genuine affection, that pushes me to broach a touchy subject.

'You know... if we had a baby, everything would be perfect.'

Tom turns to me and takes my two hands in his. 'Milly, I can't. You know that. Please don't keep asking.'

'But why not?'

'I've already told you – I'm scared that I won't be a good father. Not after what happened to me when I was young. It wouldn't be fair to you or the child.'

'I don't get it. You're the most loving man I've ever known. You'd make a fantastic dad. We can work through it together. Please, Tom? Just think about it. For me.'

'Maybe one day. But not yet. I'm sorry, Milly, but that's all I can offer.' He squeezes my hands. 'Thank you for always being so understanding.'

'No, you're right... It's okay,' I reply with a shrug, knowing that it would be pointless to pursue it for now. But I won't let it drop because I know he'll be a great dad. Much better than mine ever was.

I reach forwards and take a plate on which I place two crackers that I top with cheese. 'Yum,' I say after taking a bite. Although to be honest, I find it hard to swallow because my mouth is so dry. Whenever I get excited about something, I struggle to eat. I don't know why it happens, but I've been like that my whole life. Still, at least I won't end up constantly on a diet, like my mother used to be.

'Well, that's good to know,' he says, eating one of his crackers. 'You've lost a nail.' He points at my right hand.

I glance down.

'Damn. How annoying. When did that happen?'

I have short gel nails fitted because the awful taste of them stops me from nibbling mine. That's probably why I didn't notice it was missing – a longer nail would have been more obvious. I've been thinking about growing my own out, but with everything going on, the temptation to bite them again might be too great.

'Can it be fixed back on if we find it?' Tom asks. 'It could have come away while you were in the kitchen washing up. Shall I go and look?'

'No, it can't be stuck back on, so there's no point in looking. I'll book an appointment for a new set.' I know they're not cheap, but it's worth it.

'Okay. Let's finish this snack and get to bed. It's already gone ten, and I've got an early start.'

My fingers idly trace patterns on the arm of the sofa, a nervous habit of mine. Tom laughs when I do it and says I'll wear away the material because I do it so often.

'I wish you could take some time off so we can get this place sorted,' I say, gesturing around our old Victorian terrace. 'It's such a mess.' It's unbelievably close to the centre of Winchester, but we wouldn't have been able to afford it if it wasn't for the state it was in. The peeling wallpaper and creaky floorboards seem to mock us, a constant reminder of our neglected home life. It doesn't help that I've been spending so much time in Vivienne's immaculate place. Although, to be honest, while my focus is elsewhere, it might be easier not to start on it yet.

Tom's face softens. 'I promise to get started on it soon,' he says, reaching across to squeeze my hand, 'but you know what it's like.'

'Yes, I know,' I agree with a sigh. 'But do you realise that in all the time we've been together, the longest you've ever had off has been a week?'

'I'm sorry, love. I'll try to sort something out soon. Come on, let's go to bed.' He yawns.

I nod, not quite ready to sleep yet. My mind's still buzzing with thoughts of the power and control I now have over Vivienne's life. It's amazing how invigorating it is: like a drug coursing through my veins.

'You go,' I say, mustering a smile that I hope looks genuine. 'I'll be up soon.'

'Don't be long,' Tom says, leaning over and kissing me gently on the lips.

I reach out and pull him closer. 'I won't. Love you.'

'Love you more,' he says, before gently pulling out of my hug and heading out the room.

I listen to his footsteps heavy on the old wooden stairs and as soon as I hear the bedroom door close, I pull out my bag, opening it to stare at the things I've taken from Vivienne's house. My heart races as I run my fingers over the stolen items, each one a piece of the intricate web I'm weaving. I've left the sheets in a bag in the car. I'm not sure whether to dump them or to change them back some time in the future. Actually, that's a good idea. How funny would that be when she suddenly has her old sheets back? The thought sends a wicked thrill through me.

Before doing that, I need to work out how to orchestrate another meeting with her. My mind whirls with possibilities, each scenario more tantalising than the last.

My phone pings, and I nearly jump out of my skin.

Wow... It's a text from Vivienne.

Coincidence or what?

My hands tremble slightly as I open it.

> Are you doing anything on Saturday morning?
> Miles should be back and can look after Lola.

My heart races with excitement, but I force myself to wait before responding so she doesn't think I'm too keen. Twenty minutes tick by agonisingly slowly. I want her to think that I'm doing her a favour by agreeing to meet. This game requires finesse.

> That would be great. Text me when and where.

It's short and sweet, doesn't make me sound overly eager to meet, but, at the same time, sounds friendly.

I put away my bag, and shiver with anticipation. Everything's going according to plan. The pieces are falling into place with ease.

When I get upstairs, Tom's already asleep. His chest rises and falls in a steady rhythm, oblivious to everything going on around him. A pang of disappointment hits me. I'd hoped we might talk more... maybe even... But then I shake my head. No, this is better. I need to focus on my plans for Vivienne. He'll thank me in the end.

I slip into bed, my mind whirring. The cool sheets do little to calm the fire burning inside me. My life's on the up in more ways than one, and a smile plays on my lips.

My eyes close, and I begin to drift off to sleep.

Everything's just perfect.

As sleep claims me, a small voice in the back of my mind whispers a warning. But I push it away. This is my time, and nothing will stand in my way.

SIXTEEN

VIVIENNE

Saturday

I park the car in the multistorey car park in the centre of town and head to the vintage tea shop café where I'm meeting Amelia. It's close to the cathedral, in one of the many side streets, and not one I've been to before. I glance down at my jeans and pale-pink-and-white striped shirt. Do I look okay? Should I have dressed up a bit more? But why would I on a Saturday morning? And it's not like Amelia always dresses in fancy clothes.

I can't believe I'm overthinking everything already.

My heart races as I approach the café entrance. What am I going to do if Amelia doesn't turn up? Sit and have a coffee alone. Lots of people go out on their own and aren't at all bothered. It's just that I'm not one of them. It makes me feel too self-conscious. Miles loves his own company when eating because it gives him some much needed alone time and he can enjoy people watching at the same time. I get the people-watching bit, because to be honest, I do have curtain-twitching tendencies, but I'd rather not do it when sitting on my own in a café.

Perhaps if I force myself to do it occasionally, it will become easier.

I peer through the café window and let out a sigh of relief because, in the corner, I spy Amelia sitting at one of the tables. So, no need to be all pathetic about being in there alone. It looks like she's wearing casual clothes, the same as me. I made the right choice of attire, after all. Thank goodness. I straighten my shirt, suck in a breath and walk in, heading to where she's sitting.

'Hi,' I say, attempting a smile that I hope doesn't betray my nervousness.

'It's good to see you.' Amelia returns a warm smile of her own.

I immediately relax. Contacting her was definitely a good decision.

'Have you ordered?' I ask, glancing at the table but not seeing a number on there.

'No, I wanted to wait for you, so we could order together,' Amelia says.

'Right, well, this is my treat,' I say, feeling a sudden burst of confidence.

'Are you sure? We can always go half,' Amelia offers, pulling out a pale-blue purse from her large black bag.

'Perfectly sure. I was the one who asked you to meet up, so it's only right that I pay. And that's non-negotiable,' I add with a smile. 'What would you like?'

'I'll have a latte with oat milk, please.'

'What about something to eat? A cake or pastry?'

'Only if you're having one,' Amelia replies with a grin.

I was too nervous to eat breakfast, so will definitely be ordering something.

After giving my order at the counter, I head back to the table. 'I hope you like flapjacks,' I say, setting down the number I was given. 'They're home-made and looked delicious.'

'I love them,' Amelia says enthusiastically. 'In fact, they're one of my favourites.'

'Snap. Mine too.' I beam at her. 'The sweeter the better.'

I sit down and begin twiddling with the hem of my shirt, suddenly feeling awkward. Now we're here, it seems silly wanting to confide in someone I hardly know. Have I made a mistake?

'What is it?' Amelia asks, her brow furrowing.

'Umm... I'm now wondering whether asking to meet for a chat was a silly thing to do. You're not going to want to hear all my problems.' I glance down at the table.

'Don't be daft. I offered when we were in the park, remember?' Amelia says kindly. 'I'm here to listen. Whatever you say won't go any further. I promise.' She does a little cross over her heart with her fingers.

'Thanks,' I say, relaxing my shoulders and exhaling loudly. 'I really appreciate you being so supportive. But if I tell you everything, you're going to think I'm really stupid.' I look up and meet her eyes, which shine with concern. 'I mean, it's just so ridiculous when I think about it.'

'Try me,' Amelia says, offering a sympathetic look that makes me want to spill everything. 'It can't be ridiculous if it's upsetting you so much.'

'Well...' I pause as the guy from behind the counter brings over our order and places it on the table. I break off a corner of the flapjack and taste it, buying myself some time. 'This is delicious,' I say, gesturing to the plate.

Amelia picks up the flapjack and takes a bite. 'Mmm. You're right.' She nods her head appreciatively. 'Now, where were you?' she prompts gently.

I take a deep breath, steeling myself. 'I... I think I'm going mad.'

'Mad. What do you mean?' Amelia frowns and leans in closer.

'Weird and crazy things are happening to me. Do you know anything about dementia? Because I'm worried about getting it.'

'Not really. My granddad had it, but he was quite old,' Amelia replies, her expression turning serious.

I nod, a lump forming in my throat. 'It's in my family, too. My mum's mum. I've been researching, and some of the things that are happening to me...' I pause, staring directly at her. 'It's unusual for someone of my age to have it, but not unheard of. That's what's worrying me so much.'

'What's been happening?' Amelia furrows her brow again as she studies my face.

I fidget with my coffee cup, feeling exposed. 'It's just... things have gone missing or moved to a different place or changed completely. My dentist appointment was cancelled, and I don't remember doing it – but I must have, because it didn't cancel itself. I know that work's crazy busy at the moment, and I've been feeling so stretched that—'

'Have you told your husband?' Amelia interrupts gently.

I shake my head, feeling a twinge of guilt. 'Not really. Miles has enough to worry about. And he already thinks I'm a bit daft with all my worrying.'

Amelia's silent and appears to be considering my words. 'Look, maybe you are forgetting things, and things are going missing, but that doesn't automatically mean you've got dementia. There might be another reason. Like being stressed. It happens to all of us at some time or other.'

I nod vigorously, relief washing over me. 'Well, yes, I am stressed. That's the trouble with working full-time – well, almost full-time – and looking after Lola, who I love to bits, but...' I trail off, remembering their brief encounter.

Amelia laughs. 'She does seem a bit of a handful – but lovely with it, though. That's what you get when you have a clever child.'

I flush with pride. Lola *is* a very bright child, everyone says so. 'I know... but it doesn't make it any easier. And then there's Willow to consider. It doesn't help that Miles's away much of the time. When he comes home, everything's wonderful, but then he disappears off again, leaving me to cope with the fallout when he's gone,' I continue, the words tumbling out now that I've started. 'By fallout, I mean that we both miss him and it takes a while for us to perk up again.'

Amelia's face softens with understanding. 'It must be so hard for you. Don't you have any family or friends who can help?'

I shake my head, a familiar pang of loneliness rushing over me. 'Not really. None of my friends live close, and my parents are both dead. I have family up north, but no one local who can help. I shouldn't complain. I have a beautiful home and a comfortable life. There are plenty of people worse off than me.'

'If you need anything, let me know,' Amelia says, reaching out and touching my hand. 'I can look after Willow if you want some time for yourself. I can even take Lola to the park or out somewhere to give you a break.'

I'm taken aback by her kindness and tears spring up in my eyes, which I hastily blink away. I can't allow myself to break down here. 'That's really kind of you, but... but we've only just met. We hardly know each other.'

Amelia smiles, kindness shining from her eyes. 'You're right. But I really feel that we've connected. That first time we met, it felt like we'd known each other for ages.'

I smile back at Amelia, and suddenly things start to feel good. Confiding in someone has already made me feel so much better. Maybe that was all I needed – a confidante. I know we're going to become close friends. I can sense it.

We continue chatting, and the tension in my body begins to ease. Maybe I'm not losing my mind after all. All I needed was someone to talk to, someone who understands. I take another bite of my flapjack, savouring the sweetness and the moment of peace I've found in this bustling café.

For the first time in a while, I feel a glimmer of hope. Whatever's going on – whether it's stress, forgetfulness or something else entirely – I know now that I don't have to face it alone.

That, more than anything, makes me able to breathe again.

SEVENTEEN

AMELIA

Saturday

Finally Vivienne leaves me outside the café. Honestly, I thought she'd never go. She must have said goodbye and thanked me at least a hundred times. No wonder she has no friends, if she's always this pathetic. I scrunch up my face and wriggle it around. All that fake smiling has made my jaw ache.

The only reason I managed to get rid of her is because she wants to go into town to buy a few bits before going home. Rather than heading home myself, I'm following, but keeping out of the way. My eyes dart around to make sure no one notices me tailing her. But why would they? Nobody's taking any notice of us.

I glance down at my hand and the finger with the missing nail. It's annoying that my nail woman is away until next week, because the temptation to nibble on the end is strong, especially in a situation like this, when I'm on edge.

When Vivienne reaches one of the larger pharmacies, she goes inside, while I shelter in the entrance to the shop next door, waiting for her to leave. After a few minutes, she marches out onto the busy high street, appearing nervous and agitated. That's weird. What's going on? Her shoulders are hunched and her head's swivelling from side to side as if wanting to make sure no one's watching her.

I get ready to follow. But before she manages more than a couple of strides, one of the assistants from the pharmacy rushes out into the street and taps her on the shoulder.

Vivienne jumps and her whole body tenses.

I can't hear what's being said, so inch closer, straining my ears. Vivienne's hands are shaking as she opens her bag, and they both peer in. I hold my breath, watching the scene unfold like a suspenseful movie. The assistant cups her hand under Vivienne's elbow and escorts her back into the shop.

Has she been shoplifting? Surely not. It's not like she can't afford anything she wants. A mix of shock and excitement courses through me. What's going on?

I hurry into the shop and march towards where she's talking to two shop assistants. I can't make out the actual words, but can tell her voice is low and pleading.

Wow... This is great. Talk about playing into my hands.

I rush over to them. 'Is everything okay?' I ask, trying to hide the effects of adrenaline surging through me.

Vivienne flushes a deep shade of red and her eyes are unable to meet mine. 'I accidentally took some items without paying,' she mumbles, her voice barely above a whisper. 'It was a mistake. My mind was on other things. You know all the stuff that's been going on.'

A mistake, is it?

Well, it's one I'm going to take full advantage of, that's for sure.

'We have a strict no-shoplifting policy and will be calling the police shortly,' one of the assistants says, her stern voice cutting through the tension.

I step closer, my mind racing to find a way to solve this and put myself in Vivienne's debt. 'Look, she's my friend,' I plead, gesturing towards Vivienne. 'She's under an enormous amount of stress at the moment, and if she says it was a mistake, then I'm sure it was. She would never steal anything intentionally. You have my word for it. Please give her the benefit of the doubt. I'll pay for everything.' I reach inside my bag, intending to pull out my purse.

'No,' Vivienne says, her voice stronger now. She straightens her back, despite the desperation in her eyes. 'I can pay. Please, it was an honest mistake, like Amelia said. I promise. I wasn't even aware of what I was doing. I've been so preoccupied that I must have popped the things in my bag without even thinking about it.'

I inwardly gasp, realising the truth.

This isn't the first time she's shoplifted.

That's why I found the clothes stashed in the bottom of her wardrobe. I bet she stole them.

Oh. My. God. This is great.

I really have something on her now.

I bet the beloved husband has no idea his wife's a common thief. I struggle to keep the triumphant smile off my face as my heart races with the thrill of this newfound leverage.

'Wait here, and I'll ask my manager,' the assistant who seems to be in charge says.

She eyes us suspiciously before walking away, the other assistant moving closer to the door. To make sure we don't do a runner, no doubt. Not that I'd suggest we do that. There's so much CCTV around the place we'd be caught, and I'm not going to get myself in trouble for her.

As soon as they're out of earshot, Vivienne turns to me, her eyes brimming with tears. I bet they're fake. 'Thank goodness you came into the shop,' she says with a grateful smile, her voice quivering. 'I don't know what I'd have done without you here to back me up.'

I lean in close. 'What were you thinking?' I snap, wanting her to realise that her story doesn't wash with me.

Vivienne's eyes dart around nervously. 'You wouldn't understand,' she says, a guilty expression marching across her face. She wrings her hands and shifts her weight from foot to foot.

'We'll talk later. Not here,' I say, glancing around to make sure no one can hear.

After a few more minutes, the assistant returns. My pulse quickens as I brace myself for the verdict. Although whatever they decide will work for me.

'You're in luck,' the assistant says, her arms folded in front of her chest. 'My manager has agreed that if you pay for the items you stole—'

'*Accidentally* took,' I interrupt.

The assistant pauses, her lips thinning. 'Well... Yes... So you say. Anyway, if you pay for the items, it will go no further. But if it happens again—'

'Thank you so much,' Vivienne says, not letting the woman finish her sentence and letting out a long, shaky sigh. Her whole body seems to deflate with relief. 'I promise it will never happen again. It was a genuine mistake. Here.' She reaches into her bag and pulls out her phone, her fingers trembling slightly.

We walk over to the counter and the assistant rings up the items. I watch Vivienne closely as she taps her phone to pay, her face a mask of shame.

Beneath my concerned exterior, my body tingles with the thrill of excitement. This little incident has handed me a powerful secret, and I can't wait to see how I can use it.

'Don't say anything yet,' I say as we leave the shop and head up the crowded high street, passing a clown, with a crowd of people around him, doing tricks.

Nervous energy is radiating off Vivienne in waves.

'Thanks so much for your help,' she says once we're well

away from the shop, her voice barely loud enough to hear above the hum of passing traffic. 'I'll explain everything, but not now, because I must get home. Are you free tomorrow evening? Miles will be leaving for work during the afternoon. Come round for a drink after Lola has gone to bed... or I can make some supper. Please.'

How can I resist such pathetic begging? The desperation in her voice is like music to my ears.

'Sure. Is seven-thirty okay?' I ask nonchalantly.

'Yes, that works for me. Will your um... partner... husband... mind if you go out on a Sunday evening?'

'He'll be fine about it.'

Perfectly fine. If I'm happy, then he's happy. And he'll be even happier when I let him into the secret of what I've been doing. But that's not for now. Things need to progress further for that to happen.

Vivienne hurries away and I linger for a few moments, watching her retreating figure weave through the morning crowd. The glare from a passing car window momentarily blinds me, and when my vision clears, it's as if the world has shifted slightly.

I replay the scene in the store in my mind, savouring every detail of the stupid woman's discomfort – her fear, her shame. I couldn't have planned this better. I'm convinced that shoplifting is something she does regularly. Even if this is the first time she's been caught, which, judging by her face and reactions, I suspect is the case.

My mind's darting around all over the place, imagining the many ways I can use this information to my advantage and – by default – her disadvantage. Wouldn't it be awful if the *husband* somehow found out what she'd done? Perhaps I could let slip to the child and she might pass it on to her dad.

A nearby café door chimes as it opens, startling me from my reverie. I glance at my watch and turn to head home.

The morning air grows warmer, but I barely notice. My mind is alive with possibilities, each more tantalising than the last. Vivienne's little 'incident' has opened a door, and I intend to walk right through it. After all, what are friends for if not to be supportive and keep each other's secrets?

Tomorrow evening can't come soon enough.

EIGHTEEN
VIVIENNE

'Mummy,' Lola shrieks, hurtling towards me the moment I step through the front door, taking me by surprise. Her hair bounces wildly as she launches herself into my arms, nearly knocking me over and causing me to drop the carrier bag containing the *items* on the floor.

I stumble backwards against the door, catching her just in time. 'Hello, my little whirlwind,' I say, planting a kiss on her forehead and giving her a squeeze.

'Daddy took me into town, and we saw a clown in the street doing magic,' Lola babbles, gesticulating wildly, her eyes sparkling with excitement. 'He pulled a big bunch of flowers out of his hat and lots of coloured scarves from his sleeves.'

I swallow hard, my throat suddenly dry. Town? What were they doing there? Did they see me being caught shoplifting? My heart hammers in my chest as I force a smile.

'That's nice, sweetheart,' I manage, setting her down gently. 'I was in town, too, meeting Amelia for coffee. Did you see us there?' I ask casually, knowing that if they did, my daughter wouldn't think to keep it a secret. My palms are sweating as I await her response.

Lola shakes her head vigorously. 'No. Daddy had some jobs to do. I wanted to bring Willow with us, but he said she couldn't come because she can't go into some of the shops.'

'I'm sure Willow didn't mind being left here – she likes sleeping in her crate. What jobs did Daddy have to do?' He didn't mention going shopping today.

Lola's face lights up with a mischievous grin. 'It's a secret,' she stage-whispers, bringing her finger up to her lips in an exaggerated shushing motion. 'Daddy said I mustn't tell you.'

I frown, then realise what's going on. My birthday's in a few weeks. I bet he was taking her shopping for my present.

'I see. Well, in that case, I don't want to know and you must keep it a secret. Where is Daddy anyway?' I glance around the hall, wondering why he wasn't around.

Lola points upstairs. 'He's gone to your bedroom. He told me to stay here and play with Willow for a little while. I've been teaching her tricks in the lounge.' As if on cue, our labradoodle trots over, her tail wagging furiously, and I give her a quick rub behind the ears.

Perhaps he's hiding my present or wrapping it.

'Why don't you carry on playing with Willow while I pop upstairs to see Daddy?' I suggest. 'I won't be long, then we'll have some lunch.'

'Okay. Come on, Willow.' Lola runs off, with the dog happily following behind her.

I head upstairs to see Miles. There's no way I'm going to tell him what happened in town because he'll be shocked and ashamed by what I've done. And rightly so. Although not as ashamed as I'm feeling at this precise moment about being caught. I thought no one was looking. Anyone could have seen me – like someone from Lola's school, or one of the neighbours. What a nightmare that would have been.

I pause outside our bedroom door, taking a deep breath to compose myself.

'I'm home,' I call out before reaching for the handle, giving him time to hide whatever it is he's doing.

Miles is hunched over a small suitcase on our bed and he hurriedly zips it closed. He looks up, a fleeting expression of surprise crossing his face before he gives one of his killer smiles.

'Did you have a good time?' he asks, straightening up. 'I didn't expect you back so soon.'

I lean against the doorframe, studying him. There's a tension in his shoulders I hadn't noticed before. I hope it's not because he's worrying about me. 'Um... yes. It was great. But I didn't want to stay out too long, with you and Lola at home. You know, I really like Amelia. She's coming round tomorrow evening for a drink.'

Miles's brow furrows. 'Drink?'

Irritation flares at the implication behind his comment. 'I'll make some supper, too,' I add hastily. 'Don't worry, I'll only have one glass of wine, if that's what you're thinking.'

He sighs and his shoulders sag. 'It's just... I don't want to sound like a tyrant, but I don't like you drinking alone, that's all. But if you're with your new friend, then that's fine. Forget I said anything.'

I cross my arms defensively. 'You talk like I have no control over my drinking, which is totally ridiculous. Oh yes, that reminds me... The other day, Lola accused me of drinking too much wine and that's why I was losing stuff. You know that's down to you, don't you? It's not something she'd ever think for herself.'

A sheepish expression crosses his face. 'Did she? I'm sorry, I promise to be more careful about what I say in future.' He takes a step towards me, his voice softening. 'You know, I worry about everything you have on your plate while I'm not around to support you... Your work and looking after Lola. Drinking excessively isn't the answer to your stress.'

'For goodness' sake, Miles. I don't drink to excess. Why

don't you get that?' I give an exasperated sigh, pinching the bridge of my nose. So much for wanting to be with him to calm me down after this morning's debacle.

'Please don't be angry at me,' Miles says, taking hold of my hands in his. 'You know it upsets me.'

I shake my head. It's impossible to stay annoyed with him for long. 'I'm not. Shall I make us some lunch?'

Anything to put an end to this stupid conversation.

'Sorry, you'll have to eat without me. I was waiting for you to arrive home before leaving for work.' He checks his watch. 'My boss called. They need me there early. I'll grab something to eat in the canteen.'

'Oh.' I turn to leave the bedroom.

'Hey,' Miles calls out, his footsteps quick behind me. Before I can react, he pulls me into his arms. Despite my frustration, I relax a little as his familiar scent envelops me. 'Don't be mad,' he says. 'I'm doing this for the three of us, remember? It will be worth it in the end. I promise.'

I rest my forehead against his chest, listening to his steady heartbeat. 'Yeah... I know. But I miss you so much when you're away and...' I sigh, the words dying on my lips.

What's the point of trying to explain? It's not going to change anything. I've got another fifteen years of this to get through, one way or another. But at least I now have Amelia to confide in. Hopefully that will make it more bearable.

'Are we good?' he whispers in my ear, running his hand gently down my back.

I force a smile. 'Of course we are. Ignore me. Remember to let me know where you're going once you know and when you land.'

Ever since we've been together, he's been good about keeping me up to date on when he's going to come home, even though he can't tell me exactly where he is. It stops me from worrying about him... Well, a little anyway. They say that flying is the safest way to travel, but it's still a worry when your husband is up in the air more time than he's not.

Miles nods, cupping my face in his hands. He plants a soft kiss on my lips. 'Always. Now enjoy your time with Amelia and try not to stress too much.'

He picks up his suitcase and we walk down the stairs together. His whole demeanour changes when he's on the way to work. It's like he's already left for the day, and he's put us back in the 'home' box. All he's concerned with now is his next mission.

NINETEEN

AMELIA

Sunday

I'm seriously tempted to let myself in, just to see the shock on Vivienne's face. How funny would that be? But, of course, I can't. She has no idea that the key to her house is burning a hole in my bag. I chuckle to myself and then press the doorbell. Within a few seconds, I hear the patter of tiny feet. Don't tell me the brat's still up. Surely, she should be in bed by now.

The door opens, and Vivienne is there with that sickly smile on her face.

'Hello.' I smile brightly and hold out the cheap bottle of wine I picked up at the supermarket on the way.

'Mummy said I could stay up until you got here,' the child says, staring up at me from in front of her mother's legs before pushing herself forwards so she's almost on top of me.

I'd love to ruffle her hair, knowing that she hates it, but refrain.

'Lucky me,' I say instead with a fake grin.

'Will you read me a bedtime story?' the child asks.

Why the hell would I want to do that? She's not my daughter.

'Stop pestering Amelia, Lola,' Vivienne says with a shrug and a proud smile on her stupid face. 'She hasn't even come inside yet.'

'I'm not,' Lola says, stepping to the side so I can cross the threshold. 'Meelia doesn't mind, do you?'

'Of course I don't, Lola. But I don't have my reading glasses with me,' I say, sounding like an old granny. 'Can we save the story for another time? Is that okay?'

'Okaaay,' Lola whines.

'Good,' I say brightly.

'Make yourself at home while I take Lola up to bed. I won't be long. I've already opened a bottle of red, if you'd like to help yourself. It's in the kitchen.' Vivienne nods towards the rear of the house.

Like I need telling where everything is...

'Mummy drinks too much wine. That's what Daddy says.'

Priceless. I stifle a laugh.

Vivienne blushes a deep shade of red. 'Take no notice. She doesn't mean it. Come on, Lola, it's getting late and you have school in the morning. Say goodnight to Amelia.'

'No. I want to stay up longer.'

The child folds her arms tightly across her chest, but Vivienne takes hold of her arm and guides her upstairs. That's more discipline than she usually dishes out.

'Goodnight, Lola,' I call out. 'Don't forget, I'll read you a story another time.'

The child glances over her shoulder, but I don't wait for a response and instead head into the kitchen, barely able to contain myself at the drinking comment. Talk about playing right into my hands. This couldn't be going any better if I'd scripted it myself.

The bottle of wine and two glasses, one of which already

has some in it, are on the island. I pour myself a glass and take a sip, grimacing. I'm not a red wine lover and this doesn't make me change my mind.

'I hope you like pizza?'

I start, as I hadn't heard Vivienne come in behind me.

I plaster a smile on my face and turn around. 'I certainly do.' I raise the glass in her direction as if making a toast.

'That's great. I have one warming in the oven,' Vivienne says, as she walks over to the half-filled glass of wine, picks up the bottle and fills it to the top. 'Sorry, it's not home-made. I didn't have the time.'

'Pizza's totally fine,' I say.

'You sit down and I'll get it ready.' Vivienne gestures towards the dining table at the far end of the room, which already has cutlery for two set out, and I head over, watching as she grabs a couple of plates, opens the oven and pulls out a steaming pizza. She cuts it into slices, and brings it over, placing it in the centre of the table. She then sits opposite me.

The aroma of melted cheese fills the kitchen, and my stomach rumbles. I only had a small snack for lunch and hadn't realised how hungry I was.

We both help ourselves to a slice and eat in silence for a few minutes.

'How are you doing?' I finally ask, judging the time to be right. My voice is laden with sympathy – not too much, I hope, in case she thinks I'm being fake.

She stiffens. 'Oh, I'm fine.'

Yeah, right.

'Yes, but I mean after yesterday and... you know...'

'It was just an accident. A stupid and embarrassing mistake,' she says with a dismissive wave of her hand, but I catch the series of blinks. A sure sign she's lying. 'My mind was on other things, as you know.'

'Vivienne, this is me you're talking to.' I lock eyes with her. 'You can tell me I'm wrong, but from what I saw, this wasn't a one-off. Have you done it before? Have you got other stolen items hidden somewhere? Is this another a part of... how you've been feeling...?'

'No, it's not. It was an accident,' she repeats, looking down, grabbing a piece of pizza and taking a bite. She chews slowly, avoiding my gaze.

I lean forward, clasping my hands on the table for effect. 'Okay, if you say so. But shoplifting aside, I know you don't want to face what's been happening to you, but you must. I've thought about what you told me, and to be brutally honest, it's not looking good. The missed appointments, the sheets, losing things... When you mentioned dementia—'

'But then dismissed it,' Vivienne says.

'Yes, you did. But it got me thinking, and I reckon you might be right, especially as there's dementia in your family.' I pause, watching her face carefully before moving in for the kill. This is so easy. 'I researched dementia after going home yesterday, and you're correct in that it is unusual for someone as young as you, but it *can* happen. There are several case studies online and they started out like you. It's possible – more than possible – that you've got it. I'm so sorry.'

She stares at me, her eyes glazing over, the pizza forgotten on her plate. 'That's what I feared, but I've been trying to tell myself it's not true. But now you think it, too... We can't both be wrong. What can I do? There's no cure.'

I take a deep breath, to make it look like what I'm about to say is difficult – which, of course, it isn't. 'Well, you know I can't tell you what to do. But...' I allow my words to drift away.

'But what?' Vivienne demands, fear written across her face.

I draw in a breath, making sure it's loud enough for her to hear. 'I only know what I'd do in the same situation.'

My words hang in the air for what seems like ages. I want her to think she's dragging it out of me.

'What?' she finally asks, her voice cracking.

'I don't want to tell you.' I take another slice of pizza and begin to eat, refusing to make eye contact with her, so it looks like I'm reluctant to speak.

'Please... You must tell me,' Vivienne begs.

I swallow back a chuckle. Oh, well, if you insist.

'You won't like it.'

'Just tell me, Amelia. Please. I need someone objective to help. I can't go on like this.'

I meet her gaze steadily. 'If it were me... I'd get everything in order and then... then I'd disappear.'

'What?' Her face pales. 'Leave Lola and Miles?'

'Well, yes, but—'

'Where would I go? It would be the same wherever I was.'

'Yes, but does that matter? Isn't it better to be looked after by strangers you don't know or recognise, rather than... Do you get what I'm saying?' I ask, hoping she'll connect the dots herself.

Tears fill her eyes and roll down her cheeks. 'You mean...'

I reach across the table, but stop short of touching her hand. 'I'm so sorry. Maybe I've gone too far.'

'No, you haven't. But... why has it come on so quickly?' she asks, pulling out a tissue from a box in the centre of the table and dabbing her eyes.

'Maybe things were happening before. You could have misplaced things but not realised why. Or forgotten that you'd already emptied the dishwasher. Or accidentally cancelled appointments or not turned up somewhere you meant to be.' I hesitate. 'You know, sometimes it's like when you walk into a room and forget what you've gone in for...'

'Yes,' she says, nodding slowly. 'I've done that too. Perhaps a lot more now.'

'Well, no one else can decide what you should do. It has to

be your decision. But if it's progressing so rapidly...' I give a helpless shrug.

'I know,' she whispers, staring into her wine glass.

'Surely it will be better in the long run for Lola and Miles if you act now, while you actually can.'

There. I've said it. She will take the bait, up sticks and disappear from the lives of those she loves the most. Then justice will be served. An eye for an eye.

She pushes her plate away. 'I can't make up my mind just yet. It's... it's too much to think about. But I agree, there isn't much time.' Her voice quivers.

Correct. And I'm going to push you in the right direction.

'You know, you've mislaid the lunchbox once, but think of what could happen the next time? You might leave Lola somewhere and forget...' I let my voice trail off, the gravity of such an occurrence hanging in the air.

She sits quietly, a little frown creasing her forehead. 'You're right, but look, I've had enough for today. Do you mind if we call it a night? I'm working tomorrow morning. I've got to take Lola to school first, then I've got a meeting in Southampton.' She gives a helpless sigh.

'Of course. If I've spoken out of turn and gone too far, I'm sorry.' *Not.*

'No, you haven't. It's good to have someone like you who will tell me the truth. It's what I need.'

'Shall we make a time to meet up again?' I suggest, standing up and gathering the plates, which I take over to the sink.

'Yes, but let me get back to you on it,' Vivienne says weakly.

'Whenever you're ready. I'm always here for you,' I say softly.

In ways you can only imagine.

TWENTY

VIVIENNE

I stand on the doorstep and wave Amelia goodbye, watching her blue cardigan catch the light from the streetlamp beside our drive. My face maintains its friendly smile when she turns and waves, but inside, my mind is racing a million miles an hour. Amelia's visit has left me deeply unsettled. It's like when you're sure you've left the oven on, or the door unlocked, and even though you've checked it countless times, you're still not convinced.

I keep an eye on Amelia as she wanders down the drive and onto the street. Something's not sitting right but what is it? My fingers grip the doorframe until my knuckles turn white, while I try to work it out.

Our conversation at the dinner table was weird. Amelia clearly had an agenda and was trying to steer it in a certain way. She was even nervous about doing so – I saw her chewing on a fingernail on her right hand before she spoke. It's the only real nail. The rest are fake. I could tell by the difference in shape and colour. Her nerves could be because she was preparing to tell me that I have dementia, but was that really the reason?

I replay her words over and over in my mind like a broken record. She's convinced everything happening to me is a result of dementia. Is she jumping on the bandwagon because I suggested it the other day? Except she's taken it one step further and said the best solution for anyone in my situation is to opt out of my life... My stomach churns at the memory. I mean, who tells a person to leave their home and family? Especially someone they don't know very well, even if it is under the guise of offering an objective assessment.

The autumn breeze carries the scent of wet leaves and approaching rain. I shiver, though it's not from the cold. This goes far deeper.

I step inside and close the door behind me, leaning against it while I try to straighten out my thoughts. Okay, so things have been tricky, what with work being so hectic, and having to look after Lola on my own while Miles's away at work. But it's not like I haven't been doing that for years. So why is everything suddenly becoming so overwhelming?

Is Amelia involved somehow?

For a start, why did she try to convince me it would be best all round if I wasn't around? And more importantly, how did she know so much about all the different things that have been going on? More than I've let on during any of our chats.

I head to the kitchen, where my hand reaches for the unfinished glass of wine on the table. But before picking it up, I freeze. Staring at the deep red liquid in the bottom of the glass as it catches the light, a moment of clarity dawns on me.

I've got to stop drinking. I need a clear head to work this all out. I pour the wine down the sink and begin pacing, my slippers making soft shuffling sounds against the floor tiles.

First of all – I tick the point on my finger – how does Amelia know I've shoplifted more than once? She said it's obvious. But how can it be? What, is she a psychologist now?

Secondly – I tick my finger again – I know I told her things, but the dishwasher? I stop dead in my tracks, the refrigerator humming quietly behind me. Did I specifically mention that? I close my eyes, trying to remember every conversation we've had. I don't think so. I'm almost sure of it.

Willow lies on her bed in the corner, staring at me as I pace the kitchen, with concerned brown eyes. Her tail thumps softly against the cushion, offering comfort in her own way. 'Come on, it's almost bedtime and you need to go out,' I say.

She stretches lazily, and I open the back door for her to go into the garden, my thoughts still whirling around all over the place. While Willow sniffs around the garden, licking the wet leaves, my thoughts go back to when all this craziness started.

I tap my fingers against the doorframe.

Oh my God…

It happened a few weeks after Amelia came into my life. Why didn't that occur to me before?

The missed appointment. The moved photographs. The disappearing lunchbox. Not recognising the sheets on my bed. The times I could have sworn I'd left something on the kitchen counter only to find it in the bedroom. The empty dishwasher. Small things, tiny things, but still things that made me question my own sanity.

But how could she be doing all this?

I get how she knows about the shoplifting. She probably went through my wardrobe when she was housesitting and found the bag at the bottom with the T-shirt and underwear that I hadn't yet taken to the charity shop. They still had their tags on. Although I steal stuff, no way do I wear or use it. It's ridiculous, but that's how it is. I don't take things because I need them. The adrenaline from engaging in the act is a stress release. I've done it for years. But yesterday was the first time I've been caught.

Amelia could have put two and two together after seeing me yesterday.

I'll be able to tell if she did go through the bag in my wardrobe, because it was placed in a particular spot, so that Miles wouldn't see it.

I jog up the stairs to check and head for the wardrobe in my bedroom. I crouch down a little and reach for the carrier bag in the corner. But it's not in the right place. It's slightly to the left. That confirms it. Amelia has been in here. I stick my hand in the carrier and pull out the T-shirt. Something small flies out. It lands a few feet away on the floor.

I bend down to pick it up. It's a false nail. It's got to be the one from Amelia's hand. It's the same shape and colour. It would be too much of a coincidence for it not to be. That confirms my suspicion.

I replace the bag in the bottom of the wardrobe and head downstairs to the kitchen. Okay, so I know that she's seen the stuff I've stolen, but what about all the other things that have been happening?

Surely she couldn't have done them all?

I head to the back door. 'Come on, Willow,' I shout, my voice sharp with tension. The dog looks up at me, startled, then bounds over, leaves stuck to her paws. 'Have a treat,' I say more gently, reaching into the bag and offering her one. 'I'm going into the lounge to work all this out.'

My legs feel weak as I sink down onto the sofa, the familiar squeak of springs offering no comfort today. And then it hits me like a physical blow – the realisation so strong it nearly knocks the wind out of my lungs.

She made a copy of my keys.

My hands curl into fists, nails digging into my palms. She's been coming into the house and doing all these things to make me think I've gone crazy. But she was clever enough to wait a few weeks after the housesitting so I wouldn't put two and two together...

Except now I have.

I instinctively reach for my phone, planning to call Miles and let him know, but then something stops me. I'm going to sort this out myself. I don't need his help. I'll simply change the locks so she can't get in.

But as the thought enters my head, another one stops me cold. Changing the locks won't alter the fact that she knows where I live, work and where Lola goes to school... The implication sends a chill down my spine. I need to approach this differently. There's got to be a better way to stop Amelia from doing... What exactly *is* she doing?

It's not illegal to persuade someone to leave their family and ruin lives. But why is she doing it?

Has she done this to others? Is she some sort of sociopath? How many destroyed families does the woman have on her hands?

My mind races back over every interaction there's been between us. When we bumped into her at the park. Was that orchestrated? Being outside the shop when I'd been accused of shoplifting. Had she been following me and seen exactly what had happened, thinking she could use it somehow?

But why did she pick me? Was I in the wrong place at the right time? Or did she have some other criteria? Surely it can't have been the housesitting site because she was recommended by Miles's colleague... Unless she used them to find someone more suitable to torment? Perhaps Amelia saw how wound up I get and decided to take advantage.

I ought to go to the police and explain everything. But there's nothing to tell them. Nothing for them to go on. I've got to handle this myself. I can do it. I've got through worse things in the past.

My body tenses as determination slowly replaces the fear I've been harbouring.

I glance down at Willow, who wags her tail encouragingly, as if she totally understands what I've been saying. For the first time in ages, I feel clear-headed.

Whatever game Amelia's playing, she doesn't realise one crucial thing: she's just lost her greatest advantage over me – my ignorance.

PART TWO

THE COUNTERATTACK

TWENTY-ONE

VIVIENNE

I draw in a breath and glance at my watch. It's gone eleven, but I've never felt more awake. It might be different in the morning, when I need to be up early to get Lola ready and take her to school, after which I need to head directly to Southampton for work, but for now, that doesn't matter.

For the last few weeks, my entire existence has been a mammoth effort. Getting out of bed was itself hard, not to mention making Lola's breakfast, dealing with clients at work and being cheerful when Miles was home. Acting as if nothing was wrong was like being under constant pressure.

But now something's shifted.

Now I have a purpose: getting my own back on Amelia.

Just thinking about her sends a chill through my bones, despite the warmth of the living room. Such an innocent-sounding name for someone who's been disrupting my life in ways and for reasons only she can understand.

I sit there, drumming my fingers on my knees, the steady rhythm helping to order my scattered thoughts. The house feels different now that I know she's been behind all the incidents.

But where should I start? I ponder that for a few seconds

before sitting upright. It has to be the housesitting site where we found her.

The memory of finding Amelia's profile floods back. I'd been excited to discover someone who seemed to be so perfect, especially as she'd been recommended by Miles's colleague and she had great references. Her photo had shown a woman with kind eyes and a warm smile; the sort of person you'd trust instantly. And the day she turned up at our house, I felt that letting her into our lives was the right decision.

So much for first impressions...

I couldn't have been more wrong if I'd tried.

Leaving the lounge, I hurry to my study. After settling into my chair, I open my laptop, the blue glow of the screen feeling harsh in the dim room. My fingers hover over the keyboard for a moment before typing in the web address for Pet & Home Watch. Such a pleasant-looking website, cheerful colours and stock photos of happy families with their pets. Who would guess that a sociopath was lurking behind this normal facade?

I do a search for *Amelia*, but it comes up blank. There's no sitter with the first name Amelia on there. That's weird. I don't have her surname because the site doesn't include them. Now I come to think of it, her surname wasn't mentioned on any of her references, either. Why hadn't that been a red flag at the time? Why didn't I ask her for her last name before?

It's always easy to be wise after the event, but right now I feel like a total idiot for not finding out.

I decide to search by location instead, in case she uses a different name at different times. I put in my postcode and get a list of potential housesitters, but I look carefully at all the photos and none of them are her.

Where has she gone? Why isn't she on there?

I sit back, rubbing my temples.

She must have taken her listing down while she was terrorising me – didn't want to be bothered by other requests to housesit.

What was she going to do once she'd succeeded in getting me to disappear off into the sunset? List herself again and find another target? The thought of another family, somewhere, looking at her profile and falling for those kind eyes and warm smile, makes me want to vomit.

The trouble is, I can't warn any prospective families because there's nothing concrete to tell them. I still don't know why she's doing this to me. Taken separately, what she's done seems so trivial. The sheets changing colour. Items moving around. Photos disappearing. Appointments being cancelled. Nothing physically threatening, but psychologically... well, that's something else, especially as my life hasn't been plain sailing in the past.

If only there was some sort of forum connected to this site where I could ask if other people have used her and their thoughts. But there isn't. Maybe I should start one myself? Be proactive about it. But what would I write? *Has anyone had a housesitter who's not all they seem to be?* I'd sound crazy.

I sit back in my chair, running my hands through my hair in frustration at knowing so little about the woman who's single-handedly disrupted my life.

'Oh, wait a minute,' I say, sitting up straighter. Didn't Amelia say she works at a charity shop in Weeke? I can track her down there. That's assuming that she didn't lie about that, too. But why would she? She has no idea that I'm aware of what she's doing. I'll visit Weeke in the morning, after dropping Lola off at school.

Thinking about my daughter makes me wonder whether Amelia's been in her room, too, and taken stuff, or moved things around. To be honest, I haven't spotted anything different, but would I? For a start, I haven't been paying attention. Plus, Lola moves things around anyway, especially her toys.

But I'm still going to check. I jog up the stairs. Lola's door is slightly ajar, as I left it, and her little nightlight lights up the stars across the ceiling.

I stand in the doorway, watching my daughter sleep. My heart feels fit to burst at the sight of her angelic face. Her blonde curls are spread across the pillow and one arm is clutching Mr Snuggles. I walk across her room and check the window – it's locked. The windowsill is full of her stuffed-animal collection, and nothing seems to have disappeared. I head for her wardrobe next, and, after inspecting it, decide that nothing appears to be missing. Finally, I check her toy box and everything is in its usual chaos. I let out the breath I'd been holding during my inspection. Amelia doesn't appear to be targeting my daughter. What a relief.

'Mummy?' Lola stirs.

Damn. I hadn't meant to disturb her.

'Shh, sweetheart,' I say, rushing to her side and smoothing her hair. 'Go back to sleep.'

She cuddles up to her elephant and then nods off. I wait until her breathing evens out before leaving and heading back to the kitchen to regroup.

I take a glass from the cupboard and fill it with water, then lean against the counter.

Okay... I've got a plan to find her at the charity shop. And then what? Will I accost her? Will I follow her? What exactly?

I'm unsure of how to proceed.

More importantly, though, what shall I do about her coming into my home? I wish I'd bought one of those doorbell cams when Miles had mentioned it ages ago because it would be hard evidence of what she's doing. But I wasn't enthusiastic about it because it involves yet another app on my phone and I'm not great when it comes to stuff like that.

Then again, if we did have one of those doorbells, would she be brazen enough to let herself in any time she wanted to? I don't think so. She'd probably have forgotten about me and targeted someone else instead.

Well, once this is all over, I'll be asking Miles to get us one.

For now, there's no point thinking about it because we don't have a camera and she's targeting me and no one else – that I know of.

I lean against the island, drinking my glass of water, when the idea comes to me.

The baby cam.

I bought it when Lola was just born to keep an eye on her while she slept. I almost gave it away last spring while decluttering, but something made me keep it. Call it a sixth sense, or whatever.

I head for the utility room, and after searching through several cupboards, I locate it in its box. But where to put it?

My bedroom's the obvious place, because that's one of the places she's been. Once in there, I position the camera carefully behind a photo on the windowsill, making sure the door can be seen. If she steps even one foot in here, there'll be evidence which I fully intend to use.

I sit on the end of my bed, a feeling of uncertainty rushing over me.

What on earth am I doing setting up surveillance in my own bedroom and preparing to catch someone who might not even be doing anything?

Except I know she is.

I know this is happening, and I know that I'm not losing it. I'm not.

I can't fathom why she's targeting me. It can't be for anything I've done because we'd never even met before. It could just be down to my bad luck. Amelia clearly has some sort of psychological problem.

Does that mean she's dangerous? Am I putting our lives at risk by not telling Miles or informing the police? Amelia has had ample opportunity to harm us, if that's been her plan. This is just some sort of sick game she's playing. She wants to destroy our lives from the inside. She wants my family to implode.

I pull out my phone and check the baby cam's feed. The image appears, clear and crisp, showing my bedroom in full colour. The familiar space looks different through the camera's lens.

Now all I have to do is wait.

Wait for the woman who's trying to destroy my life.

TWENTY-TWO

AMELIA

Monday

I stretch out in bed, my arm jerking slightly, and reach for my phone to check the time. It's gone seven. But I'm not going to work today. I'm pulling a sickie because there are other things I want to do – mainly piling on the pressure to ensure Vivienne takes off, never to return.

Finally, it's eight-thirty, and I call the office.

'Napier United Pensions Company, how may I help you?' the receptionist answers in her usual jolly tone.

'Hello, Gemma. It's me, Milly. Sorry, I'm not feeling well and can't come in today. Please can you let them know in the office,' I say weakly. 'I've got an awful migraine that came on during the night.' They know I suffer with them, so it's a perfect excuse. 'I've taken some of my pills, but they've done nothing so far. I don't think it will go until I've slept it off.'

'Oh no, you poor thing,' Gemma says, sounding concerned. 'I'll let Stephen know. I hope you feel better soon.'

My boss won't mind. Stephen's a pushover – mainly because he's the sort of person who wants everyone to like him.

Most of us think he's okay, but only because he lets us get away with so much.

'Thanks,' I say, making sure to sound pathetic. 'Hopefully I'll be back tomorrow – it's usually only a twenty-four-hour thing.'

After ending the call, I slide out of bed and head for the shower. On the way, I catch sight of my face in the mirror. The muscles around my eyes are contracting very quickly, pulling at my features. When I was a kid, the doctors said I'd grow out of the tics. They were sort of right, considering I'm much better now than when I was younger.

When Tom and I initially got together, I tried to hide them, but it was impossible, and when he did see, he told me they were cute and that I shouldn't get so worked up about them. That's why I love him so much. He accepts me for who I am.

It's hardly surprising that they're making an appearance today, though, considering how close I am to achieving my goal of Vivienne's disappearance. The excitement is constant.

So far, everything's gone to plan. In fact, I couldn't have wished it to have gone any better. The execution has been simple, clean and perfect.

I take a leisurely shower, get dressed and then check the clock. *Crap.* I need to go. I hurriedly down a coffee, not wanting to start the day without my usual caffeine fix, and drive over to Vivienne's place, where I park down the road from her house in my usual spot. I want to be there to see her leave, to confirm she's left.

A few minutes after arriving, she comes out of the house, carrying a black bin bag, with the child in tow. After seating the child in her seat, she heads around to the back of the car and opens it. She lifts the bag and puts it in inside the boot, then goes to the driver's side, gets in and drives away. I do my usual routine of waiting five minutes before making a move, in case they've forgotten something and return. They don't. I'm safe.

I jump out of the car, stroll up to the house, slide the key into the lock and turn it.

Bingo. I'm in. Again.

My first stop is her bedroom. I run up the stairs and into the room.

Oh. The bed's unmade.

That's most unlike her. Usually it looks like the covers and cushions have been ironed to within an inch of their lives to make them appear perfect and unslept in.

Is this an indication that she's finally losing it?

My hands move methodically as I take off the new sheets I'd put on there and replace them with the original set. Then I make the bed. If that doesn't make her question her sanity, then nothing will.

Next, I head down the stairs to the kitchen. Beside the fridge stands the remains of the bottle of wine we were drinking last night. Hmm. Interesting that she didn't finish it. I'm about to pick it up when the sound of the dog moving in her crate disturbs me.

'It's only me, Willow,' I say softly. 'I'll get you a treat.' I run to the utility room, grab a chicken stick, and push it through the bars. The dog's like my best friend now. In fact, if they want to rehome her after Vivienne's left, then I'm first in line, providing she gets on okay with Mink the cat. I'm sure Tom would love her.

I return to the bottle of wine, open it, spit inside and replace the screw cap. After giving the bottle a shake, I place it exactly where I found it. *Gross.*

I know this won't add to Vivienne feeling that she's going crazy, but who cares? She deserves it after what she did.

Does the guilt keep her awake at night?

It should do.

Actually, it's ridiculous how easy it's been to get Vivienne to play into my hands. When I began, it hadn't entered my head that I could genuinely tip her over the edge and make her leave. At first, all I wanted to do was give her a taste of her own medicine. Make her feel isolated and desolate. But it's taken on a life of its own that's better than I could have imagined.

I glance at a photograph of Vivienne and her daughter on the windowsill, walk over and pick it up.

'You'll be better off without her,' I whisper to the little girl, my words punctuated by a sharp inhale of breath. 'Everyone will be.' My hands shake slightly as I place it back, but angling it slightly differently to how it was. Just enough for her to notice. Just enough to make her question herself. Again.

I check my watch. It's time to leave.

My facial muscles contract and release as I close the front door behind me and walk casually back to my car. Just another person going about their day. Nothing suspicious.

I start the engine, a smile on my face. Vivienne made her choice back then. Now she must live with the consequences.

TWENTY-THREE

VIVIENNE

A knot forms in my stomach as I pull up outside the charity shop in Weeke. So much is hanging on this and my nerves are shot. I get out of the car and go to the back to grab the bag of clothes I'd packed earlier. I want to have a legitimate reason for being there, so it looks like my questions are simply an afterthought.

Through the shop window, I spot a woman at the back, arranging clothes on hangers. Not Amelia. My heart sinks a little, but I push open the door anyway, triggering a small bell.

'Good morning,' the woman says warmly while walking towards me.

'Hello, I've brought in some clothes.' I hold out the black plastic bag in my hand.

'Thank you,' the shop assistant says with a smile, taking it from me.

My fingers drum against my thigh as I build up to my real purpose. 'While I'm here... I wondered... my friend Amelia mentioned working here. At least I think this was the shop? Is she coming in today?'

The woman's brow furrows. 'No, we don't have an Amelia working here. Hasn't been one since I started...'

Damn. I force back a frustrated sigh.

'That's strange. I was sure she told me this is where she works. Are there any other charity shops nearby that I could try?'

'Ours is the main one in this area, although there are several closer to town,' the woman says, peering into the bag I gave her. Then she pauses, her face brightening. 'Oh. You don't mean Milly Wade, do you?'

My heart thumps so hard in my chest I have to take a deep breath to steady myself.

Amelia. Milly... Surely that's her.

'Petite with a short pixie haircut?' I check, proud of how casual I sound.

'Yes, that's her.' The woman nods.

I want to punch the air, but, of course, refrain.

'That's great. When is she next working?'

'She doesn't work here anymore,' the woman says, looking guilty. 'I should have mentioned that sooner.'

'No problem,' I say, leaning against the counter, aiming for nonchalance. 'We haven't been in touch for quite a while – that's why I thought she was still working here.'

'Milly was only here for a couple of months when she first moved to the area. She left for a full-time office job. I can't remember the name of the company she went to, but I think it might be something to do with pensions? She said it was mainly for the money. Being a charity, they don't pay very well here. Plus, she was only working part-time. She's a very nice girl. A bit reserved, but we got on very well once the ice was broken.'

'She did enjoy working here,' I say, wanting to make out we were fairly close. 'I've had a few family issues recently, which is why I dropped the ball with keeping in touch.'

'Oh, I'm so sorry. Nothing too serious, I hope,' the woman says.

'It's fine,' I say, waving my hand dismissively. Not wanting to tell even more lies, because they'd probably trip me up. 'You don't, by any chance, have Milly's contact details, do you? I've got a new phone, and the contacts didn't transfer over for some reason and now they're lost.'

The woman doesn't look like a techie, so hopefully she won't realise I'm making this up.

'Well, I'm really not meant to – because of data protection, you know,' the woman says, hesitating as she glances around the empty shop conspiratorially. 'But, although I can't give you her phone number, I don't suppose it hurts if I say Milly and her partner bought a terraced house near Cromwell Road.'

No, it certainly doesn't hurt. Not one bit.

'Thanks so much.' I reply, trying not to sound too eager. 'That's very kind of you to tell me. It might help me find her.' I flash a smile in the shop assistant's direction and then leave for the car.

I can't follow up on any of this yet because I'm due in Southampton for work. But first, I need a moment to collect myself. I also want to check the baby cam – although I doubt there will be any movement there yet.

I pull out my phone to check the security-camera feed.

The image in front of my eyes makes my blood run cold.

Amelia's been in my house.

Ten minutes ago, she was in my bedroom.

Sheets are screwed up in her hand and the bed's fully made, which it wasn't when I left home earlier.

I stare at the screen, hardly daring to breathe, even though I know it's a recording and she can't see me.

Part of me wants to laugh – not from humour, obviously, but out of the pure absurdity of this horrendous situation I've found myself in, none of which is my fault.

I can't believe that all this time I've been seriously wondering about my sanity. The missing items, the moved furniture, the feeling of things being slightly off. And now it turns out I wasn't imagining any of it. That there's nothing whatsoever wrong with me. I'm as sane as the next person... I glance again at Amelia in my bedroom. Well, maybe not every person. I continue watching with horror as she moves efficiently around my room, like she belongs there.

My mind races through the options open to me.

The most obvious one is to phone the police. It makes sense, except I'd have to explain everything to them, and when they speak to Amelia, she might twist it around and make it sound like I've given her permission to go to my house and show them the key she has. She might tell them it's another indication of me having mental-health difficulties. She could suggest I have early-onset dementia and tell them we've spoken about it.

And what proof do I have that she's wrong? Because it genuinely seems like that's my issue.

So, if the police are out of the question, I have no option other than to continue handling this myself.

My resolve hardens.

I'll message Amelia and suggest we meet up again. Except this time, things will be very different. This time, I'll know exactly what I'm dealing with.

My fingers hover over the phone screen. The camera feed continues to show Amelia moving through my room with disturbing familiarity. She opens the wardrobe and pulls out a dress, holding it against herself. What if she goes over to the photo and finds the baby cam? My heart's in my mouth as I wait to see if she does. But she doesn't. She then heads over to the bed and adjusts the position of my bedside lamp.

I look away, unable to watch any longer. After a few seconds, I glance back and see her leaving the room. Maybe I should get another camera and position it downstairs, to give me a full picture of what she's doing?

I'll send her a message. Will that creep her out if she's still in my house?

> How's it going? Any chance you can meet up on Saturday afternoon? Lola has another birthday party, so I'll be free for a couple of hours.

I read it three times before sending, making sure it sounds natural. Casual. Like I don't know she's been standing in my bedroom, touching my things and invading my space.

She replies almost instantly.

> Vivienne. Was just thinking about you. Yes, of course. Just say when and where.

Bitch. Of course she was thinking about me. She was in my damn house.

I expect playing this game of cat and mouse gives her a thrill. Even if I didn't realise until recently that I'm the mouse.

> Let's meet at two in the park close to where I live. At the bench where we bumped into each other a while ago. We can walk and talk.

I hit send and within a couple of seconds, she replies.

> Looking forward to it. 🩶

The heart emoji makes my skin crawl. How dare she behave like this? She'll regret it. And I mean that, more than anything I've ever meant before.

I return my focus to the present and start the car, pulling into the traffic and heading in the direction of Southampton.

My mind's already on our meeting on Saturday. I've got a little over four days to prepare. There'll be no more confusion and self-doubt because I now have evidence, and more importantly, I have certainty. Amelia has no idea that her carefully constructed facade is about to crumble.

TWENTY-FOUR

AMELIA

Saturday

I head into the park, leaves crunching beneath my feet. The mid-afternoon sun brightens the scattered clouds overhead, and a mild breeze stirs the branches. I scan for Vivienne through the mix of families and dog walkers. It seems like forever since Monday when I was last in her house. Not that it matters. The seeds I've planted are growing of their own accord. I'd planned on another visit during the week, but it turned out my boss wasn't very understanding about me being off sick on Monday. It seems there's some sort of restructuring going on in the company and his position might be made redundant. I don't know why me being off *sick* is going to add to his problem, but according to him, it did.

I spot Vivienne on the weathered wooden bench near the duck pond, her head bowed. Her pale-blue cardigan makes her look washed out against the backdrop of trees. I suppress a smile at the thought of what's going to happen. She has no idea what's coming.

Plastering on my concerned-friend expression, I approach, my footsteps deliberately heavy on the gravel path. 'Hello.'

Vivienne glances up, smiling weakly. 'I'm so pleased to see you. You must think I'm awful, always moaning and carrying on, but you're the only person I can talk to. You seem to understand what I'm going through.'

I drop down on the bench next to her and rest my hand on her arm. 'Of course I don't think you're awful. You need a friend, and that's what I'm here for.'

'Thanks so much. You're an angel.'

Oh, for goodness' sake... Pass the bucket, someone.

'So Lola's at another party then?' I chuckle.

'Yes. Her social life's better than mine these days. She loves going, and it gives me a couple of hours on my own. Although whether that's a good thing when you think about...' Her words trail off.

Come on, finish the sentence... or shall I do it for you? *When you think about going craaazzzzyyyyy.*

'So your husband isn't around then?' I ask, forcing myself to focus.

'Miles is flying somewhere. I've no idea where.' Her voice wavers. 'That's part of the problem. I'm on my own so much of the time. It can't be good for me.'

'It must be really hard.' I twist the silver ring on my little finger absentmindedly, watching her face for signs of distress. 'Having Tom around—'

'Your partner? That's the first time you've told me his name,' Vivienne says, interrupting. 'Are you married, if you don't mind me asking?'

Damn. I hadn't meant to mention Tom. Not that knowing his first name is going to matter. It won't make a difference to my plans.

'It's complicated,' I say, then catch myself. I'm revealing too much. 'Anyway, we're not here to talk about me. Tell me what's been going on with you this week.'

'Shall we walk?' Vivienne suggests, standing. 'Might as well get some exercise.'

We head towards the path that circles the lake. There aren't many people close to us, and we're silent for a while. Glancing at her face, it's obvious how unsettled she is. It won't take much to finally tip the balance. Which means it's time to move things along.

'Well,' I gently probe. 'Are you going to tell me?'

'It's happening again,' Vivienne says, stopping and turning to face me. 'Nothing seems right. Things are changing... And going missing. I mean, you'll never believe this. I don't know if I told you, but I thought my sheets had changed colour, and now they've changed back.'

'What do you mean?' I ask, proud of how my voice holds steady. The sheets were inspired, if I do say so myself. The kind of subtle manipulation that makes someone question their very grip on reality.

'You're going to think I'm going insane.' She pauses and lowers her head as if embarrassed to speak. After a few seconds, she looks up at me. 'You see, I had some white sheets on my bed, and then one day, they looked like they changed to a creamy colour. Except this week, they've suddenly gone back to the old colour. It's crazy. Isn't it?'

'Hmmm,' I say, frowning. 'Are you sure they didn't change colour in the wash? Did you wash them with some darker colours? I hate it when I do that,' I say, enjoying watching her unravel.

'No, that's not what happened. The sheets were actually on my bed when they changed colour, and then on the bed again when they went back to the original.'

'Could it be the light coming in through the window at different times of day?' I say, offering another suggestion.

She glares at me. 'No. I'm not that stupid. Listen to me.' Her hand shoots to her mouth. 'Sorry, I didn't mean to snap at you. I'm grateful for your support. Coping with all this, and being cheerful all the time when Lola's around, is so very hard.'

I bet it is.

'It's fine,' I say, with a wave of my hand. 'No need to say sorry. I totally understand.'

Vivienne gives a loud sigh. 'Thanks. You're such a good friend. I can't get it out of my head that I'm getting dementia. Tell me the truth. I'm right, aren't I?'

I pause, as if choosing my words carefully. 'Look, I'm sorry, Vivienne. I can't disagree with you. I'm not a medic, so you don't have to take any notice of my opinion... but like I said the other day, you know, there are so many things pointing towards it. And it can come on quickly, like it's doing for you.'

Is that enough? I don't want to push it.

'I don't know what to do.' Her voice cracks. 'Miles is away all the time, and what if I accidentally do something to hurt Lola? I'd never forgive myself.'

My pulse quickens. She's exactly where I want her. 'Remind me, who in your family had dementia?'

'My grandma.'

'According to what I've read, it's not hereditary, but there can be a predisposition in families...' I leave the words hanging.

She's beginning to spiral, exactly as planned.

'So what shall I do? I keep thinking about what you said the other day, about taking off before it takes hold. But it's not easy. And if I do decide to go, should I tell Miles and Lola, or just disappear? If I do tell Miles the real reason for me leaving, he probably won't let me. Miles is like that – he's so caring – but how's he going to do his job and take care of me and Lola at the same time? It's an impossible situation.' Vivienne closes her eyes for a few seconds, as if processing everything.

'In that case, perhaps you should take off without telling

them,' I suggest after a while, my words like honey-coated poison.

'But where will I go?'

'Somewhere nobody knows you. Abroad. Spain, maybe?' I suggest softly, watching my words sink in like barbs.

'You make it sound easy. But my life would be over without Miles and Lola in it.'

Perfect. I suppress a shiver of excitement. We're so close.

'I don't know what to say, Vivienne. You must make the best decision you can and think of those you love. It's their lives that count now.'

'Yes, I suppose you're right.'

Vivienne lapses into silence as we walk together. My heart is racing with barely contained triumph. This is progressing way better than I'd imagined. Soon she'll crack completely, and then... adios.

I glance at her profile, noting the grimace on her face and the slight tremor in her hands. Every small sign of her deterioration is like a personal victory.

The silence between us stretches as we complete our circuit of the lake. I let it linger, knowing how uncomfortable these quiet moments make her now. She's jumping at shadows and questioning her own mind. Soon she'll be gone, leaving behind her perfect life, her perfect house and her perfect family.

TWENTY-FIVE

VIVIENNE

'Bye, and thanks again. I really appreciate you taking the time to be with me and being so supportive,' I say to Amelia with a grateful smile in the sweetest voice possible after our walk as she escorts me back to my car, which is parked close to the park's entrance.

'No problem. I'm happy to help,' Amelia replies, leaning in and giving me a hug.

It takes all my resolve not to grab her arms, wrench them off me and slap her face hard for good measure.

How dare she behave like this, the scheming, conniving bitch.

I open the car door and slide in, clicking my seat belt in place. I'm totally amazed at my acting ability during our time together. Somehow, for the entire time, I managed to remain friendly and hide the anger bubbling in the pit of my stomach. And I must have been successful, because she certainly seems convinced that I believe it's dementia that's making me like this.

I glance out of the car window at Amelia, and she smiles and waves before walking away. I sit perfectly still, intently watching her. My heart pounds against my ribs as she turns down a side street. *This is it*. My chance to find out where she lives.

Starting the engine, I slowly ease forward. Luckily, there's no other traffic, so I can go at my own pace. I turn the corner and watch as she stops halfway down the street beside an old maroon VW Golf. I pull into a parking spot and pick up my phone from the passenger seat to take a photo of the number plate when she pulls away. Then I follow at a careful distance.

At the main road, she indicates left. I keep back, not wanting to be too obvious. I know the road she lives in, because the woman in the charity shop told me, but I want to find out which house is hers. I'm not sure why yet, but know that the more I discover about her, the more in control I'll be. As they say, knowledge is power.

My thoughts go into overdrive as I follow, replaying everything the woman's done over the last few weeks. The more I dwell on it, the more disgusted I become that someone can behave in such a manner to anyone, let alone a virtual stranger.

My grip on the steering wheel tightens as I ponder who'd want to destroy someone's life like this. It's not like I know her or have ever come across her before. She's younger than me, too. So, what are the chances of our paths crossing? What could I possibly have done to her to warrant this?

A part of me wants to believe it's just bad luck she chose me, and it could have happened to anyone, but this feels too calculated and too precise for it to be coincidental. But then... Oh, I don't know, nothing about this makes any sense.

Finally, Amelia turns into Cromwell Road. My foot presses on the brake pedal as she pulls into a parking space three quarters of the way down. By some miracle, there's another spot near the top of the street, and I drive my car in. She gets out of her car, crosses the road and unlocks the door to one of the terraced houses.

'Got you,' I mutter, giving a fist pump.

The house looks perfectly ordinary from the outside: red brick, green door in need of painting, right on the pavement. But my skin crawls thinking about what might be happening behind those innocent-looking walls, the sort of Machiavellian planning being undertaken.

I glance at the car clock. It's time to collect Lola. But that doesn't matter, because I've got what I came for: Amelia's address.

As I'm about to drive away from Cromwell Road, my phone rings and the display shows Miles's name.

'Hi, you,' I answer quickly, unable to keep the happiness from my voice.

'Hello to you, too. You're sounding... different. Is everything okay?'

'It certainly is. I'm having a great day.' I grin – not that he can see it.

'That's great. What's happened to warrant this?'

I can tell by the tone of voice he's not totally convinced. Does he think this is a precursor to me breaking down?

'Oh, nothing. I've been reflecting on my life and realise how lucky I am. I don't want to take any of you for granted.'

'Oh,' Miles says, a note of disbelief in his voice. 'Well, good. What have you been doing today?'

'I've been for a walk with Amelia in the local park and now I'm about to collect Lola from the birthday party she's attending.'

'So you're still seeing the housesitter, then?' His words are slow and clipped, each syllable weighted with a pause that makes the question feel more like an indictment.

Weirdly, I'm overcome with the desire to tell him to mind his own business, but I don't, because I know exactly what I'm doing. He'd understand if he knew.

Instead I say, 'Yes, why?'

'You've suddenly struck up a friendship with her, and it

seems to have got very deep, very quickly. It's most unusual for you. You've never been like that in the past. I think you should be careful, that's all.'

He's not wrong.

'The trouble is, I've got no friends close by, and my life's taken up with work and Lola, especially as you're never here. Amelia lives in the area, so it's easy for us to get together.'

I didn't mean to rub in the fact about me being on my own all the time – it's not like he doesn't already know. And let's face it, I was the one to buy the house after falling in love with it, knowing that it meant I was isolated from people I know.

'Okay, if you're sure,' Miles says, still sounding a little upset by it. 'I don't want her taking advantage of you, that's all. You're not buying her meals or anything else, are you?'

Now's my chance to tell him the truth, and the thought fleetingly crosses my mind, but I decide against it. If he knows what I'm doing, he'll only worry. I'll tell him once it's over.

'She's not taking advantage, I promise. I did buy us coffee and a flapjack the other day, but that's it and she'll buy the next time we meet in a café. Anyway, that's enough about Amelia. When are you coming home?'

'Hopefully, I have a few days off next week. Expect me sometime on Tuesday, or possibly Wednesday.'

'Fantastic. How long will you be here for? Maybe we can go somewhere. I'll take some annual leave from work.' I sound like an excited child – which is exactly how I feel.

'I don't want to commit to anything because you know how things crop up at the last minute. We'll play it by ear, so don't mention it to Lola, in case it doesn't work out.'

'I won't. Fingers crossed, we'll see you soon. Love you.'

I end the call and feel lighter... more determined. My life's on the up now and that means Amelia's – or Milly, or whatever she's really called – is on the way down. She's about to find out what it's like when someone fights back.

My phone buzzes with a text and I glance down at the screen. It's from her.

> Let's catch up again soon. We can keep talking things through.

Why? So she can hand me a plane ticket to get me out of the country?

I smile at the screen, but it's not the anxious, forced smile of the past few weeks. Now it's the smile of someone who's gaining the upper hand and intends to make the other person pay. I type my reply and hit send.

> Sounds great. Thanks.

I'm letting her think she's still pulling all the strings because that way she won't see me coming. I need to decide exactly how I'm going to get my own back, though, and put an end to this once and for all.

I leave Cromwell Road and drive to the house where Lola's birthday party's being held; I feel energised. Everything's different now. While Amelia thinks she's orchestrating some elaborate plan to destroy my life, she has no idea I'm ten steps ahead of her. I know where she lives and now I want to find out where she works because every piece of information obtained is another card in my hand. The funny thing is that she doesn't even know we're playing this game because she's too involved in one that is indeed well and truly over.

The sound of children's laughter and chatter spills out from the house as I walk to the door to collect Lola. The other parents are arriving too, chatting about the party and weekend plans, living their normal lives. Something that I've been unable to do recently.

Lola comes rushing to the door with a party bag clutched in one hand and a half-eaten piece of birthday cake in the other, the rest of it plastered around her mouth. We go back to the car and she's full of excitement about the games they played. I listen attentively, asking all the right questions, playing my role as a devoted and loving mother.

And I am devoted, which is what Amelia clearly doesn't understand. She's trying to destroy someone who has everything to fight for.

TWENTY-SIX

AMELIA

Sunday

I stand in the doorway watching Tom, who's at the sink washing up after we've eaten dinner, choked with emotion. I'd do anything for this man, who's changed my world beyond recognition. I walk up behind him, sliding my arms around his middle, and give him a squeeze. I breathe in his scent, savouring his presence. My mind flashes back to that night he told me about the destruction of his family. The pain and torment in his eyes, when he shared the story of how Vivienne Campbell single-handedly ruined his life, will stay with me forever.

That's why I want to exact revenge on her. Not for me – for him. It's what he deserves. I love him with all my heart, and that's why I'm doing it.

Tom doesn't know of my plans to bring Vivienne down. For two reasons: first, if it doesn't work out, I don't want to disappoint him, because that might depress him even more. Second, he might try to stop me, and that would be wrong. What I'm doing is the best way for him to overcome his past.

Sometimes, I like to imagine Tom's face when he discovers

that I've put to bed the horrors he was forced to endure when he was young. Hopefully then, he'll be able to move on and we can have the life together we both deserve. Maybe he'll even consider us starting a family. That would be the perfect ending to such a traumatic story.

'I thought we could go to the movies next week?' I say, keeping my voice light.

He turns around to face me. 'Sure, that would be great. Anything in mind? Let me guess... a rom com? I know how much you love those ridiculous happy endings.'

His eyes glaze over with that familiar distant look he gets when he thinks back to his earlier life, which was anything but happy. It's the same look he had when he finally opened up to me about his past, and Vivienne's part in it. I'm sure he only told me because he'd been having nightmares where he'd be shouting and crying. It was heartbreaking to witness, which is why I'm determined to do something about it. Some wrongs need to be put right. And this is one of them.

'Actually, I was going to let you choose,' I counter. 'You do realise that happy endings are possible. Just because we both had it tough as kids doesn't mean our futures can't be good.'

'Tough? You don't know what tough is, Milly. You had a proper family growing up, and that makes a massive difference.'

I let out a bitter laugh. 'If you can call it that. You know how I always felt in the shadow of Genevieve. Having an older sister who's cleverer, smarter, more attractive than you and can do no wrong in my parents' eyes made me feel like they didn't really want me the whole time I was growing up. I was an afterthought... an accident – they told me that. For them, it was all about their precious first-born. My sister.'

'That doesn't mean you understand what happened to me.' His voice takes on that edge it gets when he talks about his past. 'You weren't moved from pillar to post in a variety of foster homes, some of which you wouldn't even leave a dog in.'

Because of what Vivienne did.

Anger flares inside me.

She destroyed everything.

But I keep my face supportive. 'Yes, but you got through it. You worked hard, went to university and got a first-class degree. Much better than my third-class,' I add quickly, seeing his guarded expression.

'There's more to life than that, Milly. Surely, you understand.'

He clearly isn't going to budge. But I do get it. Whatever he thinks, I do. I understand what it's like when your whole life is one big mess. I just wish he'd let me in.

'Do you regret moving here and living together?' I ask, my stomach twisting. I couldn't bear it if he wants to cut and run. I never question him about his previous relationships because I'm sure that's what he's done in the past, even if he hasn't outrightly said so.

'No, of course not.'

I give a sigh of relief. 'Good.'

'This house was a sound investment. Once we've done it up, we'll sell it and buy something better.' His voice takes on that practical tone he uses when he wants to end a conversation. 'You've seemed very preoccupied recently.'

'Have I? I'm not sure why,' I say, allowing myself a small smile, thinking of my plans.

He returns to doing the dishes. Will he be angry when he discovers what I'm doing? Hopefully not. Hopefully, he'll understand that someone had to make that woman pay for what she did to him and his family. And then he'll realise that what I'm doing will be the making of us.

TWENTY-SEVEN

VIVIENNE

Monday

I sigh and roll my shoulders while staring at Amelia's house from where I'm parked a little way down the road. Should I be calling her Milly, now I know her real name?

No, I can't. The name doesn't sit well on my tongue. It feels too familiar... too friendly. I'll stick to Amelia, which is distant – just like our relationship has become. I still can't believe I fell for her kindness and support, when all the time she was plotting my downfall.

Earlier, when dropping her off at school, Lola asked when we'd be seeing Amelia again because she'd promised to read her a story. I had to explain that it probably wouldn't happen for a while, making the excuse that she was busy with work. In reality, it will never ever happen. I won't let that woman within one hundred yards of my daughter. And that's a promise.

I'm determined to discover where Amelia works, which is why I'm sitting in my car observing her house. I need to know everything about her. That way, I can find something fitting to exact my revenge.

My fingers drum against the steering wheel as I wait for her to leave. The rhythm matches my heartbeat, quick and agitated. The leather of the steering wheel is warm under my fingertips, and I catch myself chewing the inside of my cheek, an old habit from childhood that surfaces when I'm deep in thought. I hope she hasn't called in sick, or is working from home. I can't stay here all morning. I have work myself, but luckily I'm not in the office today, which gives me some flexibility.

I still have no idea why she's doing this to me. Other than she's a psychopathic bully. These thoughts bring back memories of my time at school and those whispered rumours, even though I'd done nothing to deserve them. It took years of therapy before I could talk about the damage. I never thought I'd be dealing with this kind of malicious behaviour as an adult, too.

For whatever reason, after Amelia visited my house, she believed me to be a soft target. Someone she could use to fulfil her sadistic tendencies. Maybe she was right; I do have issues that make me more vulnerable than lots of other people. But why would she housesit as well as work? Unless she needs money? And if that's the case, why did she leave the website? The pieces don't quite fit together... It's like a jigsaw puzzle with edges that have been deliberately bent.

I straighten in my seat, adjusting my rear-view mirror even though it doesn't need it.

There's only one way to deal with a bully, and that's to bully them right back. Give them a taste of their own medicine. But my retaliation isn't going to be overt. I'll be subtle, so she's unsure what's going on and be unable to defend herself.

It's like a game of chess. You don't announce your strategy at the beginning of the game. Instead, you make small, calculated moves until suddenly... checkmate. Let's see how she feels when her world is spinning out of control and she has no way of stopping it.

Amelia's front door opens, cutting into my thoughts, and

she walks out. I sink lower in my seat, although it's unlikely she'll see me from that angle. Her moves seem carefree, like she's happy with her lot. But how dare she appear so calm when she's turning my life upside down?

She heads to her car, and once she drives off, I follow her through the town centre, maintaining a careful distance. Three cars between us; that's safe enough for her not to notice me.

The morning traffic is heavy, as usual, and I'm ready to follow when she signals left into the Winnell Industrial Estate. She then turns right onto one of the side roads and parks in one of the spaces belonging to a Napier United Pensions, according to the large sign on the side of the building.

So the woman in the charity shop was right about her working for a pensions company. The brick building isn't huge, and it has a row of pot plants filled with red, pink and white geraniums along the front. It seems at odds with the industrial surroundings. Judging by the size, there can't be too many people working there, which goes in my favour. Things can't be hidden so easily in a small office, and it's there that I'm going to begin my counterattack.

Once Amelia has entered the building, I leave and drive back through town, my mind already racing ahead to the next phase of my plan. I park in one of the short-stay car parks and walk with purpose towards the high street and one of the florists. I don't go to Vincent's Flowers because I often use them to send flowers to members of my team on their birthdays, or if we have a celebration. I can't risk being remembered for the order I'm about to place.

I head down one of the side streets and push open the door of Petals & Posies, a small shop with condensation-frosted windows. I've passed it hundreds of times but have never gone inside because I've always used Vincent's.

There's something fitting about that, though. New plans require new places.

A bell tinkles as I enter, and the sweet, heavy scent of lilies mingles with the sharper smell of fresh greenery. The air is thick with moisture from the flower coolers that run along one side of the shop. Buckets of flowers line the opposite wall. There are roses in deep crimson and pale pink, some bright daffodils and a bucket of orchids.

An older woman looks up from behind the counter. Her hands are stained green from stems, and she has the weathered look of someone who's spent years working with flowers.

'Good morning,' she says warmly. 'How can I help?'

'I'd like to send a bouquet.' I keep my voice light and casual, as if what I'm doing is nothing out of the ordinary. 'Something special.' My heart is pounding, but my voice doesn't waver. I'm getting so good at this deception.

'Of course. We have these charming arrangements.' She gestures to a book of examples, the pages slightly water-stained from constant use. I flip through slowly, considering each option carefully and how suitable they would be.

Finally, I point to an elaborate display of white lilies. 'This would be perfect.'

'Is it for a funeral?'

'No,' I reply, frowning. 'Why?'

'Lilies are traditional funeral flowers.'

Good. It will have a double meaning. I'd chosen lilies because they're the embossed flowers on my sheets, but I like how they can also signify the death of her plan to metaphorically kill off my family.

Will she get the meaning behind them?

'Oh. I didn't realise. But I'll still take them because my friend loves them so much.'

'Would you like to add a message?' the assistant asks.

'I'll write it myself, if you don't mind.' I print the words in careful capital letters, making each stroke precise and unfamiliar. I'm not sure if she'd recognise my writing, but don't want to risk it. She might have come across it when she searched through my house.

After asking that the flowers are delivered to Milly Wade at Napier United Pensions, and giving Amelia's phone number in case of delivery issues, I pay with cash, so there's no paper trail that connects me to it. I refrain from rubbing my hands together in glee – even though I want to – in case the woman in the shop thinks it's odd. I don't want to raise any suspicions because Amelia may very well pay a visit here to find out who sent the flowers. Well, if she does, she won't find out much.

The bell chimes again as I exit the florist and step back into the morning sunshine, feeling more positive than I have done in a long while.

I drive home anticipating tomorrow's delivery. I imagine her face when she receives them, and the way her confident smile will falter when she reads the card, unsure who sent them and why. Will she contact her partner and ask if they were from him?

I'll contact her after the delivery. Will she confide in me? How funny would that be? I glance out the window at the blue sky and shining sun. Things are on the up, and I'm feeling very positive.

Soon Amelia will know what it feels like to be on the receiving end of something that turns your world upside down. She'll understand that she picked the wrong person to mess with. I might come across as weak, but when my whole existence is threatened, all bets are off.

Do I feel guilty about turning the tables on her? In the past, maybe. But that was before someone tried to systematically destroy my life for no reason.

I unlock my front door, already planning my next move. Because this is just the beginning, Amelia. Just. The. Beginning.

TWENTY-EIGHT

AMELIA

Tuesday

I lean over my desk and rub my eyes. God, this is so boring. My fingers hover over the keyboard as numbers blur across the screen, and let out a frustrated sigh.

'Just another thrilling Monday,' I mutter under my breath, shifting in my fancy ergonomic chair that's anything but comfortable and seems to make my back hurt even more, especially after sitting in it for longer than an hour. I know that you should move around every hour, but it's frowned upon if we keep getting up to walk around.

I never wanted to be a data-entry clerk. I mean, is it anyone's ultimate career goal? When I was a kid, I really wanted to be a vet. God knows why, since I'm not great with animals. I think it was watching *All Creatures Great and Small* on TV. But I was no good at science at school, so no way was that going to happen. To be honest, how I ever passed my exams and went to university is anyone's guess. Although my university wasn't exactly a top one, unlike the one my sister went to – mine's currently rated in the bottom five of the UK's league tables. But I've got a degree in communications and it looks good on my CV.

The only thing I've ever excelled at was drama. My school drama teacher wanted me to apply to RADA, but I didn't have the confidence, and there's no way my parents would have let me. It wasn't academic enough. A wry smile crosses my face. Even without professional training, my ability to act has been useful. Look at the way I've successfully fooled Vivienne and kept Tom in the dark.

I shake my head and return to staring at the screen, trying to focus on the columns of figures that have been entered. It amazes me that I don't make more mistakes than I do because my mind wanders so much.

'Milly,' someone calls from across the office.

I turn around and see Joe, one of my colleagues, walking towards me. His face is split with a grin as he struggles with an enormous bouquet of white lilies.

'Yes?' I say, straightening in my chair.

'These are for you.' Joe's eyebrows waggle suggestively.

I swallow hard. 'For me?' Who would be sending me flowers? Unless it's Tom... but he rarely gives me flowers, and never at work.

This makes no sense.

'Someone clearly thinks a lot of you. Lilies aren't cheap,' Joe says with a wink.

I plant what I hope is a natural smile on my face. 'Thank you – they're beautiful.' My hands tremble slightly as I examine them.

'There's a vase in the staff room,' says Chloe from the next desk over, leaning forwards with interest. 'I'll get it for you.'

'Thanks,' I manage, my throat suddenly dry.

'Ooh, someone's popular. Secret admirer, Milly?' Sarah – who's been in with Stephen and has just come out of his office – joins in.

'It must be Tom,' pipes up Dean from IT, who's supposedly here to fix Chloe's computer but seems more interested in office gossip. 'He's your partner, right?'

I force a laugh. 'Yes, he is. But this isn't really his style.'

Damn. Why did I say that? Now they'll be even more curious.

Something feels off about this.

Chloe returns with the vase, setting it on my desk with a flourish. 'Come on then, what's the occasion?'

'It's a mystery man, I reckon,' Dean says. 'What does the card say?'

'I don't know yet,' I say, trying to keep my voice light as I reach for the envelope with my name on it. The handwriting is unfamiliar, all printed caps. But that was probably the florist.

'Well, open it,' Sarah urges, perching on the edge of my desk.

I stare at the envelope and eventually slide out the card and read it. The message makes my blood run cold.

I'M WATCHING YOU.

'What does it say?' Chloe leans in, but I turn the card over and slide it back in the envelope.

'Oh, just a private joke,' I say quickly, forcing a hollow laugh. 'It was Tom after all. You wait until I see him.'

'Romantic devil,' Joe says with a wink, but I barely hear him.

It's clearly not Tom. No way would he write those words. Unless he meant them in a positive way, like he can't keep his eyes off me?

But that's ridiculous.

These words are menacing, *not* endearing.

'Let me help you arrange them,' Sarah offers, already reaching for the flowers.

'No,' I say too quickly, then soften my tone. 'I mean, I'd like to do it myself. But thank you.'

I busy myself placing the flowers one at a time into the vase, grateful for something to do with my hands. The lilies smell overwhelmingly sweet, almost sickeningly so.

'They're beautiful,' Chloe sighs, continuing to peer over into my workspace while Dean fixes her computer. 'Some girls have all the luck.'

'Yes.' I manage a weak smile.

But not this time. Because something about this is wrong. So wrong.

Finally, my colleagues drift back to their desks, though I can feel them watching me curiously. Dean lingers by Chloe's computer, obviously hoping for more drama.

Once I'm alone, I open the card again. The words seem to glare up at me accusingly. Who's watching me? Are they trying to tell me something? Could it be that they know about Vivienne?

No.

This is something else. Something I could well do without. I have too much going on, as it is.

I slip the card into my bag, my mind racing. Shall I call Tom and ask him directly if it was him... to double-check? But if he says no, he didn't send them, which surely he will do, then he's going to suspect I'm seeing someone else.

'Everything okay, Milly?' Chloe asks, frowning. 'You look like you've seen a ghost.'

'Fine,' I say brightly. 'A bit of a headache, that's all. I hope it's not another migraine.'

I try to put the flowers to the back of my mind and concentrate on entering data, but my eyes are drawn to them, their presence becoming increasingly ominous in my mind. If it isn't Tom – which I'm 99 per cent certain it isn't – then could someone from work have sent them? But why? What have I done? Apart from taking time off when not really sick. Oh... and there was the time that I shared some gossip with Sarah about Chloe that turned out not to be true. And I did snap at Dean that time. But everyone acted surprised at me receiving the flowers. Then again, they would, if they're trying to wind me up.

The only thing calming me down is that I can check with the florist on my way home to find out who sent them. Once I know who, then it won't be a huge leap to discover why.

Am I overreacting? Paranoid? It wouldn't be the first time.

Maybe this is a joke played on me by someone I know? Except I'm not laughing.

Deep down, I know it's not. Someone's sending me a message.

But who? And more importantly, why?

The lilies seem to be watching me silently from their vase as I try to focus on my work, their sweet scent a constant reminder that someone out there has something on me. The question is... what?

TWENTY-NINE

VIVIENNE

I finish the set of accounts I'm working on – despite being unable to focus and continually checking the time for the past few hours – and glance at the clock on my desk. It's three minutes past two. It's time. The flowers I sent should have been delivered by now, with their cryptic message. Are they sitting on her desk right now, taunting her the way she's been taunting me?

My body tenses as I reach for my phone. Not from fear, but from a complicated mix of eager anticipation and lingering hurt. The memory of Saturday afternoon and Amelia's condescending smile while she tried to convince me to leave my family keeps entering my mind.

Who does that to someone? I still can't wrap my head around it.

Especially as she had no idea I was fully aware of her intention as we walked around the park. I shudder to think what might have happened if I hadn't discovered her plan. Would I have gone along with the idea of leaving because it would be best for me and my family?

It beggars belief that someone would suggest that, unless

they were some sort of sociopath or psychopath. I'm not sure of the distinction, but she clearly must fall into one of the categories. No right-minded person would engage in such behaviour.

I press Amelia's number, and after several rings, she answers.

'Hello?' Amelia's voice is strained and distant.

'Hey, Amelia. It's me, Vivienne. I hope I haven't caught you at a bad time,' I say, layering my voice with so much artificial sweetness I can practically taste it – and it's sweet, like justice.

'I'm at work, actually…' There's a rustling sound in the background, like she's moving papers around as if to prove her point.

Has she been staring at the flowers, trying to make sense of the message?

How poetic that for once, she's the one scrambling to understand what's going on and not me.

'Oh, sorry. Yeah, I forgot about that. I just wanted to say thank you so much for Saturday. What you said makes total sense and it has helped me clarify things in my mind. What you were saying… Well, I'll be honest with you, it was hard to hear initially, but after giving it some thought, I know now that you're right.'

I press my fist against my mouth to keep my voice steady and sounding serious. I wasn't lying because everything does now make sense, just not in the way she'd intended.

'Oh. I see,' Amelia says, now suddenly appearing much more interested in what I'm saying.

I lean back in my chair, twirling a strand of hair around my finger.

'I'd really like if we could meet again to talk some more. Maybe you can help me put things in place. There's a lot to consider. Are you around sometime during the week, by any chance?'

'Yes, I think I can do something, but I'm a bit busy at the

moment. Can I get back to you later? I'll send some times that might work.' Amelia's voice has that unsettled quality I was hoping for.

'Oh yes, of course. I'm so sorry for bothering you at work. Is everything okay?' I ask, injecting concern into my voice.

'Yes, why do you ask?' Amelia replies, sounding even more distracted. I picture her eyes darting between the flowers and her computer screen, trying to maintain her composure and be friendly towards me.

'You're sounding a little off. Is it something I've done? Tell me to back off if there's a problem – I don't want to overwhelm you with my worries when you're obviously preoccupied yourself.'

I can do emotional blackmail as well as the next person.

'No, no,' Amelia says quickly, too quickly. 'Something's cropped up at work, that's all. Look, I'm sorry, I didn't mean to take it out on you. I promise I'll get back to you later today and we'll sort out a time when we can meet up again.'

I decide to push harder and not accept her answer, especially as it's obvious that she's already off-balance.

'Well, you'll never believe it, but Lola's got yet another party to go to this Saturday afternoon, and Miles isn't around – as usual. If you're okay with it, why don't we meet then? I'm a sure a few more days won't make any difference.'

It gives me a chance to do something else to her that will put her on edge. How funny would it be if she starts to confide in me, thinking that I might be able to help her?

'Yes, if that's okay and you don't mind waiting until then, that works for me,' Amelia says.

'As long as Tom won't mind.' I'm almost tempted to suggest she bring him, too, but she'd know something was wrong if I did. Although, I must admit to being curious about the man she's with. Does he know what a deranged person he's living with?

'Why should he?' Amelia snaps, then audibly sucks in a

breath. 'Sorry, I didn't mean to say it like that. He'll be fine about it.'

'That's great. I'm sorry for calling while you're at work. I hope you won't get into any trouble for taking a personal call.' My voice drips with pseudo-concern.

'They'll be fine. It's just that I've got a lot on, and it makes it hard to chat,' Amelia replies, her voice still sounding guarded. 'I'll call you tomorrow to make plans.'

'Okay, that's fine. We'll decide where to go then. And again, thanks so much. I can't begin to tell you how much I appreciate you being here for me.' I struggle to keep the triumph out of my voice.

Although I suspect it's more relief than triumph.

'You're welcome. Sorry about snapping before. You know I've always got time for you.'

And she expects me to believe that?

'Thanks, I appreciate it.'

After ending the call, I spin around in my office chair and smile to myself. But it's a complicated smile because although I've now got Amelia on the back foot, that doesn't mean her vendetta against me is over. Despite what's going on, it wouldn't surprise me to learn that she's already working out what to do next.

I'd hoped she'd mention the flowers, as they'd only just been delivered. Did they make the impression I wanted? From our conversation and how distracted she sounded, it certainly seems that way. I imagine her fingers tracing the edges of the anonymous message, trying to work out who sent it, and why. Or maybe she gets the meaning – that she's going to get what she deserves – but she just doesn't know how yet.

Satisfaction spreads through me like warm honey. The pieces of my plan are falling into place one by one, and she's dancing to my tune without even realising it, all the time believing she has the upper hand.

Maybe, just maybe, after this is all over, she'll understand what it feels like to be on the other side of someone's victimisation. Not because my sole goal is to hurt her, but sometimes the only way to stop someone like her, whether a psychopath or not, is to show them their own reflection.

THIRTY

AMELIA

Every minute of this afternoon has seemed like an hour. Finally, with only a quarter of an hour to go, I start packing away my things, knocking over a pen holder in my haste.

Not that I managed to get much done after those stupid flowers arrived. They're sitting on the desk mocking me, beautiful and threatening all at the same time. Their sweet scent has been making me nauseous all afternoon.

My stomach churns as I glance around the office. I've been continually thinking about my colleagues, trying to work out who sent the flowers. I could make a case for each one of them. The message 'I'm watching you' is so pointed. It's got to be from someone who thinks I've done something wrong.

The only person I know who didn't send them is Tom. I'm convinced of that. He's never cryptic. If he has something to say, he'll come out and say it. That's because he's had it tough and come through the other side... Well, almost the other side. And after I've finished with Vivienne, he really will be able to put it behind him.

To be honest – although I would never say this to him –

sometimes I think he had it better than I did because he was able to be whoever he wanted without trying to please everyone. Which isn't an easy situation to be in. A bitter laugh escapes me as I remember my past.

I gather my belongings, nearly dropping my phone in my haste. I'll find out one way or another who sent me the flowers and confront them. It's not going to be hard to discover because I know exactly where the florist is and I'm heading straight there. A rookie mistake on the sender's part, if you ask me. Providing the florist is still open when I get there, it won't be long until the sender's identified.

I hurry out of the office without waiting for anyone else – as normally I would – and soon I'm driving into town. After parking in one of the car parks, I head for Petals & Posies, the florist. I breathe a sigh of relief when I get there, because it's open until six. My heart's pounding so hard I can feel it in my throat.

I push open the door, forcing a bright smile onto my face. The shop's small, and the heavy scent of flowers and damp soil hit me. Metal buckets line the walls, bursting with roses, carnations and seasonal blooms in clashing colours that make my already anxious head spin. The whole place has a shabby, lived-in feeling that usually wouldn't bother me, but today it feels suffocating.

'Hi,' I say, trying to keep my voice steady.

'Can I help you?' a woman standing beside the counter asks.

'Yes, I hope so. I received some flowers today that, according to the packaging, came from you. I know who sent them. Well, I'm almost sure... but I don't want to thank them in case it wasn't them and it causes a problem.' I shrug and give a small laugh. 'The trouble is, they didn't sign the card under the message. I think they might have forgotten. Is there any chance you can tell me who sent them, please? They were delivered to me at work. My name's Milly Wade.'

'Hold on a moment and let me have a look,' the shop assistant says as she opens a book on the counter.

How old-fashioned. Don't they use a computer?

The woman flicks through the pages and frowns. 'I'm sorry, I can't tell you who sent them because they paid in cash.'

My stomach drops. Bloody hell.

'Didn't you take a name from them?'

'No, we only take the recipient's phone number in case we're not able to deliver.'

I sigh loudly. 'Well, do you remember taking the order at least?' Surely she would, considering it's such a small shop.

'Sorry, this order was taken yesterday morning and I only work in the afternoons. My colleague Fi, who was working yesterday morning, might remember. It just depends on how busy she was. Monday does tend to be hectic because we have a lot of deliveries.'

My heart sinks even further, and I lean against the counter to steady myself. 'What about CCTV?' I ask, sounding hopeful.

The woman laughs. 'We don't have anything as advanced as that. We're just a small florist and those systems are very expensive. All I can think of is you say thank you and see what happens? Otherwise you might not find out.'

I sigh. I'd already told her that wasn't a good thing to do. But clearly she wasn't listening to me.

'I'd rather not do that unless it's a last resort. When will Fi be working again?'

'She'll be here tomorrow morning.'

Damn. My anxiety spikes at the thought of asking for more time away from the office. I can't.

'Oh. That might be difficult. And after that?'

'Fi's working tomorrow morning and then she's off for a few days, but she'll be in all day Saturday, if that helps. Maybe you could pop in then and see if she remembers? I'll leave a note to let her know you'll drop in.'

'Would you? That's so kind. Thanks. I can definitely call in then,' I say with a smile.

'Saturday's usually our busiest day, so I'm not sure whether she'll be able to spend too much time with you, though,' the woman adds.

'I totally understand. I'll try Saturday first thing and promise not to keep her long. Thank you so much for your help – it's very kind of you.'

I leave the shop and lean against the window, my legs feeling weak. How on earth am I going to last until Saturday before finding out who sent the flowers?

It's the same day that I'm seeing Vivienne again. At least that's something to look forward to. My hand goes to my throat and I massage the tight muscles there. I'll have to be careful what I do at work from now on, in case someone there is after me. Because one thing's for sure, I don't want to lose my job, in case I can't get another one. If that happens Tom won't be happy. He's always had a thing about someone wasting their day doing nothing when they could be out doing something productive. I think one set of his foster parents sat on their arses all day, taking money from the government for fostering kids and really doing nothing for them. He complained to the social workers, and they moved him on. Maybe he should've put up with his foster carers, then he might have been able to stay in one place instead of constantly moving.

As I walk back to my car, every member of staff at Napier United Pensions becomes a suspect. Could Sarah from HR have sent the flowers? Or maybe it was someone from accounts. What if this is only the start of something bigger? Does this mean I'm going to be walking on eggshells all day, every day while I'm at work? The possibilities swirl in my mind like leaves in a storm.

I fumble with my car keys, dropping them twice before I

manage to unlock the door. And as I sink into the driver's seat, I catch a glimpse of myself in the rear-view mirror. The strain's already showing. I don't need it. I have other, more important, things to deal with.

THIRTY-ONE

VIVIENNE

Thursday

I sit back in my desk chair, its familiar creak matching my sigh of frustration. The last two days have dragged like crazy and I've heard nothing from Amelia. My fingers tap against the polished wood of my desk as I ponder our last conversation a few days ago when I phoned her at work. She said she'd call yesterday, but I never heard from her. And so far she hasn't contacted me today either. Surely she'd want to if she has her own agenda regarding our relationship?

Maybe she's too preoccupied with the flowers to contact me. That's got to be good because it means I'm getting to her... Even if she doesn't know it's me, yet, behind her distress.

I can't rest on my laurels. I need to keep up the pressure.

So, what to do next... what to do next...?

I tap my chin with my finger while thoughts circle my mind like a hungry shark until... *wait*...

I've got it. This one will cut her to the core.

My pulse quickens as the idea takes root and I chuckle to myself. If this doesn't do the trick, then nothing will. My fingers fly across the keyboard as I search the internet for one that's suitable. And there it is – it couldn't be more perfect.

The gift message option catches my eye. My hands hover over the keyboard as I consider my words carefully, wanting to compose a message that's going to knock her for six.

The wrapping paper I select is cream with gold ribbons. Professional. Tasteful. Poisonous.

I pause, my finger hovering over the *Place Order* button. Lola's school photo catches my eye from its place on my desk, and my stomach tightens. What exactly am I working towards here? The endgame is still frustratingly unclear.

I could expose her publicly and lay out her destructive behaviour for everyone to see. But would that be enough to stop her? And more to the point, would the public humiliation make her even more dangerous? I have my family to consider. Nothing is as important as they are. However much I want Amelia to suffer.

Maybe a private confrontation would be better. Just the two of us, with all my evidence spread out between us like playing cards. I could demand she puts an end to the persecution and threaten to expose her if she doesn't agree. Or even threaten to go to the police and say she's been stalking me.

But what if Amelia cornered turns out to be Amelia at her most volatile? For all I know, she might turn violent and direct it at my family, as well as me.

There's always the option of taking this to her boss at work – not that I know who they are, but it won't be hard to discover. Then again, this isn't anything to do with work. What about Tom, her partner? I could approach him and explain what his girlfriend has been doing and ask him to stop her. But would he believe me? And what if he's somehow involved? He might know what she's been doing and encouraging her, thinking it amusing.

It's a real conundrum. And I'm not sure there's a right answer. For now, though, sending this gift will have to do.

I'm about to enter my card details and finish the order when my phone buzzes against the desk. The screen lights up with Amelia's name.

Speak of the devil.

I open the text.

> I'm fine for Saturday afternoon. Shall I come to you?

Interesting. Short and to the point. Maybe more so than usual. Not that she's one for chitchat in texts.

I lean back, letting the chair's support catch me as I weigh my options. Do I want her in my home again? The thought of it gives me the shivers. But then again...

Control the environment, control the game.

Where did I hear that?

I don't remember, but it doesn't matter because the saying is certainly apt.

Oh... I've had an idea. I'll put my phone on record when we're together, so if she tries to convince me to leave my family again, I'll have it documented as evidence. So whatever I decide to do next – whether it's the police or Tom – that will help.

I pick up my phone, hit reply and type:

> Perfect. See you Saturday. Come after three-thirty – I'll be back from taking Lola to the party then.

After sending it, I return to the online order and double-check every detail before finalising the purchase, paying extra for next-day delivery. I'd give anything to see Amelia's face when she opens the package. Will she open it in front of her colleagues, or maybe do it surreptitiously, after remembering the flowers?

I'd love to conveniently drop by her office just as the gift arrives and watch her reaction with innocent eyes when she opens it. Okay, I know that's not possible, but the thought of it causes my expression to brighten.

How's she going to process it? Who will she blame? One thing's for sure, it won't be herself. She'll probably sit there feeling like a victim. Not that it matters. This is just another step in my plan to bring her down.

My fingertips trace the edge of my desk as I consider what to do after the gift has been delivered. Should I contact Amelia, or wait until she visits on Saturday afternoon? That way, she'll have had plenty of time to stew on it and wonder who's targeting her. She might even begin to accuse people. That would be interesting to watch.

The afternoon sun slants through my study window, casting long shadows that seem to dance with possibility. I'll admit that the ending may not be clear yet in my mind, but each little event I orchestrate brings me closer to figuring out exactly how I want this to play out.

THIRTY-TWO

AMELIA

Friday

'Look who's Miss Popular again.' Chloe bounces over to my desk, her ponytail swinging with each step. She's waving a small, brown package in her hand and is practically vibrating with excitement. I force myself not to roll my eyes at her ridiculous behaviour. She needs to get a life if she thinks me receiving something in the post is worth getting excited about.

Despite that, my stomach twists into a knot and acid burns at the back of my throat. Surely this isn't another 'gift' from whoever sent the flowers. I resist the urge to shrink back in my chair and straighten my spine so as not to give away my anxiety.

'This was delivered to reception and Gemma asked me to give it to you.' She thrusts the small box towards me, her perfectly manicured nails contrasting against the cardboard.

'What is it?' I ask, taking it from her.

The fluorescent lights suddenly seem too bright, too harsh.

'We won't know until you open it,' Chloe says, leaning against my desk and staring at the package.

I glance around and see Joe staring in my direction, too.

Sarah also peeps up from behind her screen. All we need is Dean to make a show, and it's a full house.

And then he walks into the office. Typical.

Being the centre of attention means I have no choice but to open the package. My fingers tremble slightly as I open the box and discover something gift-wrapped. I unwrap the cream-and-gold paper, the soft whisper of expensive wrapping feeling somehow ominous. A silver handle emerges first, its ornate scrollwork catching the light. My fingers still as they reveal the rest. It's a vintage handheld mirror with an elegant oval frame. Its pristine surface reflects my pale face as I read the message on the card.

Karma's a bitch

'What is it?' Chloe leans in, her floral perfume over-whelming me as she tries to peek. Her shadow falls across the damning mirror.

'Nothing,' I snap, slamming the mirror face down on my desk with enough force to make my water bottle topple over. 'Leave me alone.'

Chloe recoils as if I've slapped her, her cheeks flushing pink. Her bottom lip quivers slightly. 'Oh... okay. Be like that, then.' She stomps back to her desk, hurt radiating from her rigid shoulders, each step deliberate and loud.

Perfect. Just perfect. Now my colleagues are falling out with me too.

I hurriedly pull open the drawer and drop the mirror in there. Chloe couldn't have seen it or she'd have said something. Unless she was the one to have sent it and was just pretending to be hurt.

'What's going on? I heard shouting,' Stephen says, coming out of his office.

'Ask her,' Chloe says, nodding in my direction.

'Milly?' He strides over to my desk.

'Nothing,' I mutter.

'She received a gift and got all silly about it,' Joe says.

I glare at him. 'It wasn't that. Anyway, I don't want to talk about it.'

'That's fine, but make sure the shouting stops. This is a workplace, not a playground,' Stephen retorts.

I can't help but exchange a glance with Joe and Sarah at the sharpness in our boss's voice. It's like he's turning into another person.

'Sorry,' I mutter.

He returns to his office, and the three of us sit in silence for a few seconds.

'What's got into him?' Chloe finally says, her previous upset seeming forgotten.

'It must be the threat of redundancy,' I reply, wanting her to think there are no hard feelings between us.

'It's not that,' Joe adds. 'There's trouble at home. I overheard him on the phone to someone. It sounded like it could have been his wife.'

'We don't know for certain,' Sarah adds. 'You shouldn't be spreading rumours.'

'I'm only saying what I heard,' Joe replies. 'It's not a rumour.'

'Well, there's no need for him to take out his personal problems on us,' I say, glancing at Chloe, who rolls her eyes in my direction and then returns to her desk.

The five of us get back to work, and once I'm sure no one is looking in my direction, I carefully pull out the gift from my desk drawer. I read the message again. What does it mean and why send it on a mirror?

As if I need to ask. It's obvious they're telling me to look at myself. That what I put out into the world comes back to me.

My eyes dart around the office, studying each bent head. It

must be someone from here. I don't know anyone else. The few friends I have are all in Manchester.

Unless...

Could it be Vivienne?

But how could it? She doesn't know my real name, doesn't know where I work... In fact, she doesn't know anything about me.

I catch Sarah stealing a glance at me from her desk, her glasses reflecting the overhead lights. Dean quickly looks away when our eyes meet, suddenly very interested in his computer screen.

Oh my God. They're all watching. All of them. The walls of the office seem to close in, the air becoming thick and heavy. It's them. They're the ones trying to freak me out. They're in it together.

'Right, you lot,' I call out, my voice higher than usual, cracking on the last word. I stand up, pressing my hands flat against the desk to keep them steady. The cool surface anchors me. 'Someone's playing jokes on me and I want to know which one of you it is.'

I stare at each of them in turn, searching their faces for any sign of guilt. They look back with mixtures of confusion and concern, some shifting uncomfortably in their chairs.

'Why would we do that?' Joe asks, frowning, his bushy eyebrows drawing together.

'I don't know,' I snap. 'But it's got to be one of you.'

'It's not me,' Chloe says.

'Nor me,' Joe adds.

Dean and Sarah say the same.

But that doesn't mean they're telling me the truth.

'Okay, it doesn't matter. Forget I said anything.' I sink back into my chair.

But it does matter. Of course it does. It matters so much.

The room spins slightly, and I close my eyes, trying to steady myself.

They might deny it now, but I'll find out the truth. And once I have the evidence, the person will regret ever trying to cross me.

I pick up my phone, and, while pretending to text, take photos of everyone in the office. The only people I don't have are Stephen and Gemma, the receptionist. I'll get them later.

Tomorrow morning, I'll visit the florist and show her photos of everyone here. I know it's one of them. Surely with a photo in front of her, she'll recognise who came in and ordered the flowers. Then I'll know who's got it in for me. And once I do, they'll regret it. One hundred per cent.

THIRTY-THREE

VIVIENNE

'Come on, sweetheart, it's time for bed,' I say to Lola as she sits cross-legged on the floor in her favourite unicorn pyjamas, completely absorbed in the cartoons on the telly, her little face lit up by the bright colours. My heart swells at the determined set to her chin and the way she wrinkles her nose as she's about to protest. But forewarned is forearmed and I brace myself for her tantrum. The more tired she is, the more she tries to fight it.

'I'm not tired, Mummy. Please let me stay up a bit longer?' She yawns and turns to me with those big, brown eyes that, unless I'm strong, will get her exactly what she wants. A ridiculous situation to be in with a five-year-old. But with everything else going on, sometimes I let her get away with things I shouldn't.

'It's getting late, and you don't want to be tired tomorrow for the party,' I say, hoping that will persuade her.

'But Daddy's going to phone soon and I want to speak to him,' Lola says, her face scrunched up in a frown.

My heart squeezes a little. Miles should have phoned by now. I suppose he's been held up. That's what often happens. 'He might have been delayed at work. Let's go upstairs and I'll read you a story. If Daddy phones once I'm back down here, I'll come straight up to your room, and if you're awake, you can talk to him. Promise.'

I watch the internal debate playing across her face and stay quiet until she responds.

'Okay,' Lola finally says, sighing dramatically as she stands up. 'If you promise.'

Her mannerisms remind me so much of my mother that I have to stifle a laugh. She heads towards the door, dragging her blanket behind her like a mini queen reluctant to leave her throne.

I follow behind her, and we're about to leave the lounge when my phone rings. My heart skips a beat as I pull it out of my pocket and glance at the screen.

'Is it Daddy?' Lola squeals, turning to face me and bouncing on her toes with sudden energy.

'Yes, it is,' I confirm, swiping to answer and putting it on speaker. 'Hi, Miles, I'm here with Lola.'

'How are my two favourite girls?' His warm voice fills the room, and I feel that familiar flutter in my stomach. Even after all this time, he still has that effect on me. I guess that's what true love is.

'I'm going to a party tomorrow,' Lola bursts out, the excitement reverberating off her.

'What, another one?' Miles says, sounding shocked. He chuckles. 'You must be the most popular girl in your entire school. How many is that you've been to now?'

'Lots and lots.' Lola twirls around the room, her energy seemingly limitless now that she's hearing Miles's voice. 'I'm going to wear my new pink dress with gold glitter on it and the special shoes that Mummy got me.'

'You'll be the belle of the ball,' Miles says.

'And I'm giving Wilfred some Lego,' Lola says.

'Wilfred?' Miles says, sounding amused.

'It's a popular name nowadays,' I reply, suddenly feeling very old. It's the sort of thing elderly people would say.

'Oh... I see. Well, I'm sure *Wilfred* will love the present. I've got some news.' My stomach tightens at the change in Miles's tone.

'Oh... what?' I ask, holding my breath and preparing for the worst.

Will it be weeks before we see him again? This job of his seriously drives me crazy. Especially now with so much going on.

'There's been a change of plan, and there's a chance I might not have to fly this weekend.'

My heart skips a beat and I glance at Lola, watching her process this information. When it clicks, her entire face lights up, and we both break into matching smiles. My mind races with cautious optimism.

'Oh, that's fantastic.' I catch myself, not wanting to sound overenthusiastic in case it doesn't work out.

'I'll find out for definite first thing in the morning.'

'Where are you at the moment?' I try to keep my voice steady despite the anticipation bubbling up inside me. 'Sorry, I know you can't tell me.'

'Can you take me to the party, Daddy?' Lola asks, her eyes shining with possibility.

'I might not be back by then, sweetheart. But, if I'm home, I'll definitely come with Mummy to pick you up afterwards. Is that okay?'

'Yes.' Lola starts jumping around the room. 'Daddy's coming home. Daddy's coming home. Daddy's coming home.'

I watch her, my chest tight with both joy and anxiety. I know how disappointed she'll be if it doesn't work out. But it's nothing I haven't managed in the past, and I'll be able to do so again if I have to.

'How's everything with you, Viv?' Miles asks, his tone shifting to something softer.

'Everything's good. I've got something to tell you, but it can wait until we're together.'

There's so much we need to discuss – especially about Amelia – but not with Lola in the room.

'When Mummy says that, it means she doesn't want to say anything in front of me, doesn't it?' Lola asks, stopping her dancing to look up at me with an all-knowing expression.

Miles and I both burst out laughing.

'Honestly, nothing gets past her,' I say, rolling my eyes in our daughter's direction.

'Yes, it does. Lola, you're a very clever girl,' Miles says, the pride in his voice coming through.

'That's what Mummy says, too,' Lola says.

'And she's right.'

'Right, say goodnight to Daddy because it's time for bed. The sooner you go to sleep, the sooner tomorrow will come and then you have your party to go to.'

'Okaaay. Ne-night, Daddy,' Lola says reluctantly.

'Goodnight. Fingers crossed I'll see you tomorrow,' Miles says, and I can hear the mixture of promise and caution in his voice that I feel in my own heart.

Lola holds up both hands, showing her fingers crossed. 'I'm doing it, Daddy.'

'Me, too,' I say, following suit.

As the call ends, happiness radiates from Lola. She skips ahead of me up the stairs towards her bedroom, singing a little song to herself. I trail behind, contemplating tomorrow and confiding everything to Miles.

He needs to know what's going on with Amelia – that situation can't wait much longer. Although right now, everything seems more manageable and I can't help feeling optimistic that it's soon going to be sorted out once and for all.

If he's home when Amelia comes round tomorrow afternoon, we can confront her together. She'll see then that it's not just me she's dealing with.

I return my focus to Lola and tuck her into bed, watching her cuddle with Mr Snuggles. I lean down and kiss her forehead, breathing in the sweet smell of her freshly washed hair. 'Sweet dreams, darling.'

'Mummy?' Her voice is already heavy with sleep. 'Do you think Daddy will really come home tomorrow?'

I pause, choosing my words carefully. 'I hope so, sweetheart. But remember, even if he can't make it this time, he loves you very much and we'll see him soon.'

'I know,' she mumbles, her eyes closing. 'I love you, Mummy. See you in the morning.'

'Love you too, sweetheart,' I reply, my heart almost fit to burst.

Until Lola was born, I didn't realise it was possible to love someone so much. I'd do anything to protect her. Anything.

I stand in her doorway for a while, watching her finally drift off to sleep and her chest rise and fall in a slow rhythm. It's like she doesn't have a care in the world, and that's how I want it to remain.

The house feels quiet now, almost too quiet. But instead of feeling lonely, there's a sense of anticipation hanging in the air. I'm convinced that things are starting to look up and all my problems will soon disappear.

THIRTY-FOUR

AMELIA

Saturday

My hands are rigid on the steering wheel as I drive into the centre of Winchester, my mind racing with how to approach the florist and what to do with the information once I have it. I have enough on my plate dealing with Vivienne. How am I going to cope with confronting whoever it is who's trying to frighten me? Maybe I should keep the information to myself and bide my time before getting my own back. Which I will... and then some.

The traffic's light and by nine o'clock, I drive into one of the central car parks. The morning air is crisp, and my shoes thud purposefully against the pavement as I head straight for the florist. The closer I get, the louder my heart pounds, but I force myself to appear casual as I push open the door, setting off the cheerful little bell above. The sound feels almost offensive in its innocence.

A different woman to my previous visit looks up from behind the counter, her grey-streaked hair catching the morning light. She's older than the other assistant, with reading glasses hanging from a pink-and-gold chain around her neck. She sets down a half-trimmed rose.

'Good morning,' she says warmly. 'Can I help you?'

I lean against the counter, trying to appear nonchalant despite my sweaty hands and knotted stomach. The edge of the counter presses into my palms, grounding me.

'I hope so,' I say with a smile. 'Were you working here on Monday, by any chance?'

'Yes, I was.' She picks up her scissors again, returning to the red roses laid out in front of her on the counter.

My throat feels dry. 'Actually...' I glance around the empty shop, the rainbow of flowers suddenly feeling like an audience. 'I received some flowers at work on Tuesday, which had been ordered on Monday, and I was hoping you might remember who sent them?'

The scissors pause mid-snip. I watch her face carefully, noting how her expression shifts from open to guarded. 'Oh, you're the person who came in on Tuesday afternoon. I was left a message about it. To be honest, I'm not really supposed to—'

'Please,' I interrupt, lowering my voice so it sounds a little desperate while leaning in slightly. 'I just want to thank the right person. The thing is... well, the flowers were paid for in cash, and I'd hate to approach the wrong person and make things awkward between us. Surely you understand.'

The woman sets down the scissors with a clunk that echoes in the quiet shop. 'Well...'

I reach for my phone. 'What if I showed you some photos of my friends? And you can give a nod if you recognise anyone? That's all I'm asking. A simple nod won't be going against the law. Please.' My voice sounds strange to my own ears: too high, too frantic.

She glances towards the back room as her fingers nervously play with her glasses chain. 'I'm not sure. My manager wouldn't like it if she finds out.'

'I completely understand – I used to work in retail myself.' I give her my most sympathetic smile, the muscles in my face straining with the effort. A bead of sweat trickles down my spine despite the shop being cool. 'All those rules. But surely there's no harm in looking at a few photos? I mean, you're not actually telling me anything. And I promise not to tell anyone what you did.' I glance around as if checking we're alone.

She wipes her hands on her apron, leaving faint green smears. 'I suppose... What was the order exactly?'

'Flowers sent to Milly Wade at Napier United Pensions on the Winnell Industrial Estate.'

Recognition flashes across her face. 'Ah yes, I do remember now.' Her eyes light up. 'Lilies. The person who ordered them wrote the card themselves and placed it in the envelope and—'

'That's the one,' I cut in quickly, my heart hammering so hard I'm sure she must be able to hear it. I pull up the first photo with trembling fingers. 'So, this is a colleague of mine, Chloe.'

The florist shakes her head. 'No, definitely not her.'

I swipe to the next photo – of Joe – trying to keep my hand steady. 'Was it him?'

'It was a woman,' the florist says with another shake of her head.

'Her?' I ask, showing a photo of Gemma.

'No, sorry, dear.'

Each negative response increases the tension coiling in my stomach. I've run out of women at work to show her.

I swipe and a photo of Vivienne pops up. No point in showing her. But still my finger hovers over her photo.

'I know it's probably not her... but just in case.'

The florist peers at the screen and her face changes subtly. There's a slight widening of her eyes, and a barely perceptible intake of breath, but it might as well be a confession written in neon lights. Her eyes dart between my face and the photo. She gives a small, almost imperceptible nod. It's as if she's giving away some trade secret.

'Are you sure?' My voice comes out as a whisper, though inside my mind is screaming.

'Well, I...' She fidgets with her glasses chain again, clearly uncomfortable now. 'I really shouldn't have...'

'No, no, you've been incredibly helpful.' I force my lips into a smile even as bile rises in my throat. 'Actually, this is exactly who I thought it might be. Now I can thank her properly for sending such a gorgeous bouquet.'

'Oh good.' She looks relieved and returns to her roses. 'I was worried for a moment.'

'Don't be. You've done nothing wrong.' I straighten up, adjusting my bag on my shoulder. Its weight feeling like an anchor. 'In fact, you've helped me more than you know.'

'Well, that's lovely then. It's always nice when mysteries get solved, isn't it?'

'Oh yes, it definitely is. Thanks so much,' I say, already turning and striding towards the door, anxious to leave before the scream that's bubbling inside me erupts.

Leaving the shop is like emerging from underwater. The bell's cheerful tinkle follows me outside like mocking laughter, and the morning sun is so bright I squint against its intensity. I need to get back to the car before collapsing, but every step seems like I'm wading through treacle, my legs so heavy with the weight of what I've learnt.

I finally get to the car park and manage to drop my keys twice before unlocking the car. The metal feels ice cold against my fingers, despite the warm day. I slide into the driver's seat and grip the steering wheel until my knuckles turn white.

It's Vivienne playing games with me.

Is it because she's discovered what I've been doing?

Well, if it is, she's not going to get away with it.

Let her send flowers and a mirror with pathetic cryptic

messages. Let her play her little mind games. If she thinks she can intimidate me, she's got another thing coming. She has no idea what I'm capable of. Of what I'll do to protect the man I love. This isn't about petty revenge – this is about justice. About finally making her face up to – and pay for – what she did.

Okay, so I've failed at getting her to leave her family because she thinks she's got dementia. But there are plenty of other ways to make her pay for what she did. I can tell her friends. Her family. Her work colleagues. She'll be a social outcast by the time I've finished, and it's nothing more than what she deserves.

Vivienne might have worked out what I've been doing, but I bet she doesn't know why. Or how much I know about her past. And she certainly has no idea how thoroughly I'm going to destroy the careful life she's built on other people's pain.

She's expecting me at her house later when the brat's at a party. Is she planning to confront me? Or is she still going to pretend that she's losing the plot? Whatever it is she thinks is going to happen, she's wrong. So think again, Vivienne Campbell.

I merge into the stream of traffic, driving on autopilot while thinking about what's coming next. I think of Tom. Of all the therapy sessions he told me he'd been to that never quite got to the heart of the effect his past had on him, mainly because he couldn't bring himself to speak the words out loud. Even when I've tried to talk to him about it, he clams up and says he doesn't want to remember it. That his focus is on me and our time together.

Well, now that Vivienne knows what I've been doing, the time for subtle manipulation is over. Sometimes, the only way to deal with a snake is to cut off its head. And today, I'm bringing the knife. For Tom. For the boy he was, and for the man he could have been if she hadn't destroyed something precious and irreplaceable that summer.

Oh yes, Vivienne Campbell might think she's clever with her gifts and warning messages. But she's about to learn that some secrets can't stay buried forever. I've had enough of watching my partner suffer while she lives her perfect life, with her perfect husband and child, seemingly unburdened by conscience or consequence.

I hadn't expected her to discover what I'd been doing, but the tables have turned full circle. She won't get the better of me. There's no fear of that.

PART THREE

THE CONFRONTATION

THIRTY-FIVE
AMELIA

I stare at Vivienne's perfect house with its perfect garden. Okay, so I'm obsessed with everything she has being perfect... except I know that it's a facade, just like everything else about the woman. The afternoon sun casts long shadows across her fancy car. Why has she got all this, and I haven't? It's not fair. Especially after what she's done.

I haven't yet decided how to play this. It goes in my favour that she has no idea I've sussed her little game. Although, part of me is desperate to scream it in her face so I can watch her perfect mask crack and shatter. But I'm not sure that's the best plan. I need to be smart about my course of action. Strategic. Maybe I'll play it by ear. Now I'm here, that's all I can do.

I press the doorbell and wait, the chime echoing inside. She might think it's musical, but it's not. It's a warning.

I hear footsteps, and Vivienne opens the door with a smile that's so fake it makes me want to vomit. She's wearing what looks to be an expensive pale-grey cashmere cardigan, like a winter sky. It's perfectly coordinated with a pair of navy slacks. Usually she's in jeans when we meet up. Does she think I'll be intimidated by this sudden change in appearance? Well, if she does, she's even more stupid than I thought. Just because she's got more money than me, doesn't make her special.

'Hey, Amelia. It's great to see you,' Vivienne says warmly, as if butter wouldn't melt in that disgusting mouth of hers. 'Come on in.' She holds open the door and gestures for me to step inside.

I manage a tight half-smile and follow her down the familiar hallway to the kitchen, which is immaculate as usual, with gleaming surfaces and everything in its place. My fingers itch to open every drawer and cupboard and pull everything out until it's an unrecognisable mess.

'How are you doing?' I ask, fighting to keep my voice neutral even as bile rises in my throat. I thought it would be easy to maintain the facade I've been keeping up for so long, but for some reason it isn't. My fingers trace patterns on the granite worktop, leaving faint marks that fade almost immediately.

'Oh, you know. Up and down.' She gives an exaggerated sigh. Except I know it's false. 'Would you like some coffee? I bought some new beans from that little shop in town. So much nicer than instant. Or a cup of tea? Or a soft drink? It's a bit early for wine, I suppose.' She gives a chuckle, and that's enough to make something snap inside of me.

'No.' The word comes out sharper than I intend, but I'm past caring.

Let her hear the edge in my voice. Let her wonder what's going on and why my manner has suddenly changed.

She slowly turns to face me, her eyes widening in fake innocence.

'What? You don't want anything?'

A humourless laugh escapes me. 'Finally, you ask the right question.' My voice is barely above a whisper, but in the quiet kitchen, it might as well be a shout. 'No, all I want is to sort this out once and for all. I know you sent the flowers to me at work, and I assume you also sent the mirror. Don't try to deny it.'

A strange look crosses the bitch's face. One of determination and defiance.

'Oh,' she says coldly, taking a step in my direction and drawing herself up to her full height so she towers over me. 'I have no intention of denying it, because you're right, it was me. And now it's time for us to lay our cards on the table and have it out once and for all. I'll start, shall I? I only did what I did because of you,' Vivienne adds, not giving me a chance to reply to her question.

'How *dare* you try to destroy my family?' she continues. 'What the hell were you thinking when you came into my life and tried to make me think I've got dementia? I can't believe you even pushed for me to walk away from my family. My whole life.'

Vivienne folds her arms tightly across her chest and stares down at me. Her eyes are blazing, but behind them, I can see she's unsure.

Vulnerable.

Scared.

That's enough to push me into saying more.

I take a step back and lock eyes with her, refusing to be intimidated.

'It was no more than you deserve, after your behaviour. You might think it's in the past, but, believe me, it isn't. It's as fresh now as it was then.'

Vivienne's face contorts with fury, all pretence of civility vanishing like smoke.

'How dare you speak to me like that. Get out of my house. Now.' Her finger jabs at me. 'I know everything you've done to me, and be warned, if you try anything like that again, it'll be more than just me you'll have to contend with. Do I make myself clear?'

I lean forward, holding her gaze with an intensity that makes her take a step back.

'How dare me? Ha. You mean how dare *you*?' My voice comes out as a dangerous whisper. 'After everything you've done, you have the audacity to blame it all on me. All I'm doing is exacting revenge. You've got a lot to answer for, Vivienne Campbell. Your past is coming back to haunt you. No one should get away with what you did.'

'Amelia,' Vivienne says, her voice honey-sweet again as if she's trying to regain control. 'I think you're confused. I've no idea what you're talking about. You've got the wrong person.'

She stares at me, faking bewilderment.

'You know exactly what I mean. Don't lie to me,' I say, through clenched teeth.

The perfect kitchen suddenly feels like it's closing in on me, and I gasp for breath. I'm not leaving until she admits what she did.

And then what?

I don't know. My head's a jumble of thoughts.

'I'm not lying. It's you who's the liar. Who's got it wrong,' Vivienne says, the sweetness gone as quickly as it came. 'Whatever you think you have on me, you're wrong. You're the one with the problem. You think you can come here and try to destroy my life, but you're not as clever as you think. Far from it. Because I found you out. And it wasn't exactly difficult. You dropped yourself in it by saying you knew about stuff I hadn't told you, and that was enough for me to see right through you. Don't try to deny it because I have evidence which I'll use if necessary.'

Her words hang in the air, and the kitchen clock ticks loudly in the silence between us. She might think she's got the better of me, but she hasn't.

'You really thought you could get away with it, didn't you?' I shout, unable to contain myself. 'You talk about *me* trying to ruin *your* life... that's a fucking joke, because *you're* the one who ruins lives.'

THIRTY-SIX

VIVIENNE

What the hell's going on? My heart pounds against my ribs as I stare at the woman... whatever her name is. She's standing in my kitchen like an avenging angel, accusing me of all sorts. And I've done nothing.

I grip the edge of my kitchen island, grateful for its solid presence. Everything else feels like it's spinning out of control.

'Look here, Amelia... Milly,' I begin, trying to keep my voice steady, although my whole body's shaking, 'I've never done anything to you. You have to believe me. I don't even know who you are. You were the one to come into my house and do all those awful things to me. You were the one who wanted me to think that I was losing my mind.'

Something about her presence, her certainty, makes my stomach churn. I reach for my coffee cup, needing something to do with my trembling hands, but I miss and knock it sideways. Dark liquid spreads across my pristine countertop.

I grab a cloth and start wiping up the spilled coffee, focusing on the mundane task to keep myself grounded. I've always found cleaning soothing. *Order from chaos. Control.*

'No.' Her voice cuts through the air like ice. The way she's looking at me – like she can see right through me – sends shivers up and down my spine. 'You can deny it all you want., but I know exactly who you are and what you've done. And where you did it.'

'Then tell me,' I challenge, straightening up and spreading my arms wide. 'Tell me everything, because as far as I know, you're making this up. You wanted an excuse to destroy someone's life, and for some reason, I happened to be the person on whom you chose to play your dirty tricks. Did you think I wouldn't work out what you were doing? Was making me think I was losing the plot your intention the whole time?'

I stab a finger in her direction, surprised by how fierce and aggressive I sound. This isn't me... I never act like this. My hand hovers in the air between us, and I quickly lower it. A strand of hair falls across my face, and I tuck it behind my ear.

'You know what you did,' she says, her voice dropping to a dangerous whisper. 'Why should I have to spell it out to you?'

'Because if you don't, then how the hell am I going to know what you're talking about?' My voice rises until it sounds like it's bouncing off the ceiling. 'This is ridiculous. Tell me, for God's sake. Tell me. Because if you don't, then we're going to be here all day, and this will never get sorted.'

But even as I say the words, something dark and forgotten stirs in the back of my mind. Like a shadow seen from the corner of your eye that disappears when you turn to look at it. *No. It can't be.*

She takes a step closer, her eyes boring into mine. 'Try thinking back a few years, *dear,*' she says. The way she says it makes my blood run cold. 'Then maybe, just maybe, you might realise what I'm talking about. You know what happened in the past,' she continues, each word falling like a stone into the still water of my carefully constructed world. 'I suppose you've tried to bury it and pretend that you don't remember, but now it's coming out. Now everyone's going to know what a manipulative little—'

'Look, you're talking nonsense.' My voice rises an octave in pitch, verging on hysteria, as I interrupt her. I press a hand to my throat, my pulse racing beneath my fingers. 'I keep telling you, I haven't done anything.'

'You're wrong,' Amelia states, her tone icy cold.

I rake through my memories, panic rising like bile. The past feels like quicksand: the more I try to focus on it, the more it shifts and slides away from me.

'Nothing I've done has ever harmed anyone else,' I say.

But even as the words leave my lips, an image flashes through my mind...

No.

I won't think about that.

I can't.

A cold sweat breaks out across my forehead, and I reach for the counter to steady myself. Things were done to me, things I choose not to remember, but it can't be that. How can it? It was me who was harmed. No one else. And I paid the price.

The silence stretches between us, heavy with unspoken accusations. I open my mouth to say something to fill it, but my throat tightens.

Before I can force any words out, the front door slams, the sound echoing through the house like a gunshot. I nearly collapse with relief, my knees finally giving way. It must be Miles. Thank goodness. He'll fix this. Get rid of Amelia from our house forever. From my life.

The sound of footsteps in the hall feels like salvation, but as I look at Amelia's face, at the triumph blazing in her eyes, something tells me this is far from over. Whatever she thinks I've done, whatever she thinks she knows, it's about to come to a head.

But somewhere, in the darkest corner of my mind, a tiny voice whispers that maybe, just maybe, I deserve what she intends to do to me. Except I don't. It wasn't my fault.

THIRTY-SEVEN

AMELIA

Saturday

'I'm in here,' Vivienne calls out in a strained voice that sounds almost desperate.

Hardly surprising now I have her running scared. I can tell from her expression that she knows why I'm here.

I turn my head towards the sound of footsteps coming down the hall. Don't tell me this is the elusive Miles that she keeps talking about? The one I was convinced didn't even exist. After all, what kind of husband is never around? Never in any photos? It all seems really weird, if you ask me. My fingers drum against the counter, anticipation building inside me.

Now he's here, he can learn the truth about his wife. Find out what she's really like. Then let's see her try to get out of what she did all those years ago.

'Hi.' His voice echoes around the room before he actually walks into the kitchen through the door.

I freeze, my body turning to ice. That voice... it sounds eerily familiar. But surely...

'Thank goodness you're here,' Vivienne says, running over to him as he strides into the kitchen.

My jaw drops wide open.

The world is suddenly sideways.

This can't be happening.

'Tom?' I barely recognise my own voice, thin and brittle as breaking glass. 'What are you doing here?'

I look at Vivienne, who's standing beside him, confusion flickering across her face. My stomach heaves as I watch him remain perfectly still. His face is expressionless, but there's something in his eyes that I've never seen before... something cold and calculating... almost satisfied.

'What do you mean, *Tom*? This is Miles,' Vivienne says, her voice wavering slightly, as she steps back from him. 'This is my husband, Miles.' There's a desperate edge to her words, like she's trying to convince herself as much as me.

'No, no.' I shake my head violently, my voice rising. 'Why are you pretending he's Miles? Tom, tell her who you are.'

I stare at my partner, who still hasn't moved and has a deadpan expression on his face. No guilt. No shock. Nothing. Just... empty. No, not empty. It's not that. There's something else. He's watching us both like we're characters in a play he's been directing all along.

'What's going on?' Vivienne demands, her voice cracking. 'Miles, why is she calling you Tom?'

'Because that's Tom,' I burst out, forgetting the speech I'd prepared about her betrayal, because this is so much worse.

All I want – *need* – to know is why Vivienne is calling my Tom her Miles. It can't be right. Her husband's a pilot for the army. She told me that. He's away a lot of the time. Tom's a consultant, and yes, he's away some of the time—

Oh.

Oh God.

Suddenly, things start piecing together like a horrific puzzle.

The absences. The fact that he's always so busy and wanted to move to Winchester.

Tom still hasn't moved, not trying to comfort either of us.

And now I see it. The slight curl at the corner of his mouth and the way his eyes are drinking in our distress, like he's relishing a glass of fine wine. This isn't a mistake. This isn't a man caught in a lie.

This is a plan that he's been executing the whole time.

But how did he know I'd be here? I didn't tell him what I was doing to Vivienne. Has he been going through my phone and checking up on me?

My legs won't move. I want to run, to scream, to throw something, but I'm glued to the spot, my body refusing to obey as my world crumbles around me. The silence stretches between us like a taut wire, ready to snap.

'Well,' he finally says, his voice carrying none of the warmth I once thought I knew. He looks between us with something almost like amusement. 'Isn't this interesting?'

THIRTY-EIGHT

VIVIENNE

I stare at Amelia, then at Miles, my head spinning like I'm on some twisted carousel ride and can't get off. The room seems to tilt and shift, the familiar walls of our kitchen suddenly feeling alien and hostile. My stomach churns violently and bile rises in my throat as I try to process what's happening.

How can we both be sharing the same man? It makes no sense.

I taste copper. I've been biting the inside of my cheek without realising it and now it's bleeding.

I take more steps backwards and stare again at Amelia and then Miles. 'Are you two in this together?'

My voice is small, childlike even, as inside I'm screaming that this can't be happening. That I need to wake up from this nightmare.

Miles's face is cold and distant. He looks at me like I'm some stranger off the street. Someone he doesn't know. Gone is the man who phoned Lola and me yesterday, promising he'll be home soon. This version of him is a stranger wearing my husband's skin.

What's going on? Why is he doing this to me? *To us.*

My hands start shaking so badly I have to dig my nails into my palms, the sharp pain anchoring me to reality.

This isn't real.

It can't be real.

Wake up, Vivienne. Wake up.

I pinch my arm hard, twisting the flesh until I wince at the sharp pain shooting through me. The room stays stubbornly solid around me.

I'm not dreaming. I'm not.

The clock on the wall ticks away mercilessly, marking each second of this nightmare.

'What's going on?' I demand, after neither of them answers my previous question.

My eyes dart between Miles's stone-faced expression and Amelia's dazed one, searching for any crack in their facades, any hint that this is all a joke, even if I don't find it funny.

Something shifts in Amelia, like she's turning on a switch. Her spine straightens and her shoulders square as if she's preparing for battle. The confusion in her eyes hardens into something dangerous.

'I'll tell you what's going on,' she says, her voice so icy it could freeze hell. 'You did something to Tom many years ago. Don't deny it.'

The accusation hits me like a physical blow. 'What are you talking about? This is Miles, my husband.' I gesture wildly at him, my wedding ring catching the light – the ring he placed on my finger with promises of forever. 'I didn't know him years ago. What on earth could I have done to him?'

'It wasn't him you harmed,' Amelia says, her eyes flashing. 'It was his father.' She turns to Miles, and something passes between them, some dark understanding that excludes me entirely. 'Tell her, Tom. Tell her.'

My mind tries to connect impossible dots but comes up

with nothing. The walls seem to be coming in on me and I can hardly breathe. 'I don't understand...'

'Do you remember Mr Williams?' Amelia says, the name falling like a guillotine blade. 'Your teacher.'

The penny drops, and my legs nearly give out. I grab the island to steady myself. 'Mr Williams? But that's not even Miles's surname.' Even as I say it, pieces start clicking into place with sickening clarity.

'Did you or did you not accuse your teacher of sexual harassment?' Amelia demands, each word precise and cutting.

My throat feels like sandpaper. 'Yes... yes, I did.' I wrap my arms around myself, shivering despite it being a warm day. Old, unwanted memories surface and I try to push them back, but can't. 'I don't understand what's going on here. None of this makes sense.' I turn to Miles, pleading, searching for any trace of the man I married. 'Talk to me.'

But all he does is stare at me, and I finally see it... or rather, the lack of it. The warmth I thought was love in his eyes is gone, replaced by something hard and unfamiliar. Something that's been waiting, perhaps for years, to reveal itself. My mind races with horrible possibilities, each worse than the last. If he's Mr William's son, why is he with me? Has our relationship been a setup? Our marriage some elaborate plot to seek revenge? Has he been working with Amelia all along?

But then, how can it? She seems as shocked as I am that we're sharing the same partner.

'You don't understand. You weren't there at the time,' I say weakly, realising how pathetic it sounds. The magnitude of what's happening threatens to overwhelm me. My life with Miles is built on a foundation of lies.

Amelia's lips curl into a bitter smile, the kind that promises there's more pain to follow.

'Well, now you've got the chance to tell it as it really was.'

Her words hang in the air, and I realise with crushing certainty that this is only the beginning.

THIRTY-NINE

AMELIA

Vivienne stares at me, her expression determined, but also haunted. Tom stands by the door, unmoving. I don't know how this Miles/Tom thing is going to work out, but my heart pounds against my ribs. We're about to cross a point of no return, I know it.

'Okay,' Vivienne says, her voice barely above a whisper. 'Yes, I did accuse Mr Williams of being a sexual predator, because that's what he was.'

Okay, now I'm going to find out the truth.

'Liar,' Tom blurts out, the venom in his voice causing me to take a step back.

'Maybe I didn't use those exact words, which I didn't understand at that age, but it's true.' Vivienne wrings her hands together. 'He called me back after class one day. I was the only one there with him, and I knew… I knew something was going to happen. It was written all over his face.'

Her words trail off, and I turn to look at Tom's face. His features are contorted with anger and his hands are clenched into white-knuckled fists at his sides. I've never seen him like that before.

'That's not true,' he spits out. 'My dad didn't do that, you're making it up—'

'Yes, he did,' Vivienne says, cutting him off mid-sentence and meeting his gaze. Tears well in her eyes but don't fall. 'He cornered me in the classroom and put his hand up my skirt.'

'You could have stopped it,' Tom says, his voice cracking like a whip.

A bitter laugh escapes Vivienne's lips. 'I did. I tried to push him away, but he was stronger than me. He was bigger than me. I was only fourteen.' Her voice drops to a whisper. 'But he just kept coming. I was so scared but...' Vivienne lifts her chin, a flash of pride on her face breaking through. 'I stamped on his foot as hard as I could and pushed him with all my might. It threw him off guard, and then I ran out of the classroom. Told my friends—'

'That's bullshit,' Tom explodes, taking a menacing step in Vivienne's direction.

I instinctively move between them. Suddenly, I'm not sure who to believe.

'It wasn't my dad,' Tom growls. 'It was someone else. How do you know it was him? You just made it up.' His tone rises hysterically. 'You're lying. I know you are. Teenage girls are like that. Always trying to cause trouble and make up stuff that's not true.' The rambling words spill from his mouth.

'I'm not lying.' Vivienne's voice is quiet but sincere.

Tom stands there, staring at her and then at me. I can see the conflict raging behind his eyes. The desperate need to defend his father warring with the apparent truth in Vivienne's words. His world is crumbling before my eyes.

A terrible question rises in my mind: is Vivienne telling the truth? Has Tom been mistaken all these years that it was all made up? Did the attack on her by his father really happen, exactly as she said?

The silence that follows is deafening, filled with nothing but harsh breathing and the sound of long-buried truths finally coming to light.

FORTY

VIVIENNE

Suddenly, the years seem to roll away, and I'm fourteen again, standing in that classroom. The memory hits me with such force that I can barely breathe – the sound of the door clicking shut and the way Mr Williams's footsteps seem to echo as he walks towards me. I smell the chalk dust in the air and feel the edge of the desk pressing against my back as I try to maintain the distance between us. His smile changes and turns predatory. The heavy aftershave he's wearing makes me want to gag.

Don't panic. Stay calm. Someone will come in.

But nobody did. The corridor outside was empty. Everyone had gone home. Just like he planned.

I shake my head to get rid of the memory and focus on the here and now as I face his son. Miles.

All this time, I never knew... Why didn't I see it? The same height as his dad. The same way of tilting his head before he's about to speak.

Our life together – everything we've shared – has been built on a lie.

'Is that it?' Amelia's voice cuts through my thoughts, bringing me sharply back to the present.

'I'm telling you what I said is true.' I force myself to look at Miles, though it feels like my heart is being ripped apart. 'I'm sorry, Miles. I don't know what's going on here, but every girl in school knew about your dad. Everyone was warned to stay out of his way, but this time...' My voice cracks. 'I was lucky to get away, because if I hadn't...' I wrap my arms around myself, fighting back nausea. 'I swear he would've raped me. I'm sure of it.'

'And you expect me to believe that far-fetched story, do you? If everyone knew, as you say, then how come the teachers didn't put a stop to it? How come he didn't get the sack? You're talking crap.' Miles's voice is harder than I've ever heard it before.

I flinch. 'It was known around the pupils. I don't know about the staff. But I promise that it's true. I wouldn't make up stuff like that.' Tears stream down my cheeks. 'After what happened, I went home and told my parents, and then they started the ball rolling. I didn't know it would lead him to taking his own life. How could I have done?' I reach out towards him instinctively, but he recoils. 'I'm sorry, Miles. Really sorry, but your dad was a sexual predator and there's no other word for it.'

'Why didn't you say anything before? Why not share it with your husband?' Amelia asks, seeming puzzled.

'It took years for me to get over it. And I haven't really after all this time. But I've learnt to put it to the back of my mind and not think about it. I didn't want to tell him. Surely you understand that.' I glance at Amelia but can't tell whether she believes me or not.

I return my gaze to Miles, whose face is contorting with rage and his features twisting into something almost unrecognisable. 'You're lying. Stop it. You ruined my whole life.' He begins pacing, clenching and unclenching his fists. 'After what happened and he took his own life, Mum went to pieces and it killed her. I was only eleven. You don't know what it was like, being stuck in foster homes, going from place to place...'

'I'm really sorry, Miles,' I repeat, my voice breaking. 'But you can't expect me to take the blame for what your dad did. Because I'm telling you' – I press my hand against my chest, feeling my racing heart – 'it's stayed with me my whole life, even if I've never mentioned it before. I never truly trusted any man until I met you.' I laugh bitterly. 'But now I know it's been one big lie. What about Lola? When you came into our lives, was she part of your grand plan, whatever that was?'

'Isn't Lola his?' Amelia asks, who's watching us with horror.

'No. I've only known Miles for three and a half years. But he's always treated Lola as if she were his own. She'd never had a dad before, because she was the result of a one-night stand. But clearly getting Lola to think of him as her dad was part of this hideous, manipulating charade... that he loved us.'

I stare at Miles, and then look back at Amelia, my body numb.

What the hell's going to happen now?

The room seems to spin around us as years of secrets and lies come crashing down like a house of cards.

Nothing will ever be the same after this moment, and we all know it.

FORTY-ONE

AMELIA

My eyes are glued on Tom and the expression on his face. A face I thought I knew better than my own. But this... this is different. His features are strange and my skin prickles. It's like staring at a stranger. This isn't Tom. Or Miles. Or is his real name different again? If his dad was Mr Williams, then why does Tom use Tyler?

Tension radiates from every line of his body.

'The only person lying is you,' Tom begins in a low and dangerous tone. 'It's all lies.' I watch, transfixed, as his hands curl into fists. 'My dad didn't do anything to you. You were a pathetic little teenage girl wanting attention.'

The hatred in his voice makes me flinch.

'That's not true.' Vivienne's voice is steady, but I see the slight tremor in her fingers as she clasps them together. She stands her ground, though, and something about her composure seems to infuriate Tom even more.

'Yes, it is.' The words explode from him, spittle flying from his lips. His face has gone red, a vein pulsing at his temple. 'My dad wouldn't have done that. He was a good man, and a fantastic father.' He takes another step forwards, and both Vivienne and I instinctively move back. 'I don't care what you say about girls thinking he was always after them – it's all made up.' His voice rises to a shout that echoes off the walls.

'It's not, Miles. I promise it's not,' Vivienne says, her voice low.

Tears of rage stream down Tom's face, but he doesn't seem to notice them. 'You ruined my life.' His voice cracks. 'You ruined my mum's life. You ruined my dad's life.' Each accusation is like a physical blow. 'And that's why I'm going to ruin yours.'

Silence fills the air, but my mind is working overtime trying to work out what's happening. This can't be the man I live with. The man I love.

'What I don't understand is how I fit into all this?' I ask.

Vivienne's face is impossible to read as she looks at me. 'It's simple. Miles, or Tom as you know him, used you to get at me. You were his instrument of revenge.'

That can't be right. Surely, I'd have known. Tom doesn't even know what I've been doing to Vivienne. It was meant to be a surprise.

I look at Tom. 'Is she right?'

The smile that spreads across his face will haunt my nightmares forever. It's not the smile I've woken up to countless mornings over the last couple of years. It's something else entirely... something cruel, satisfied and triumphant.

'Yes.'

My brain fights against the implications, but reality is crashing in hard.

'You planned all this?' My voice rises as understanding dawns. 'You... you planned for me to come and make Vivienne think she was going crazy? But how? You didn't even know what I'd intended to do, for goodness' sake. I wanted to make you feel better, by...' My words trail off.

Tom locks eyes with me, the derision in them making me

physically recoil. He's not the man I knew. That man's gone. For good.

'Manipulating you was so easy.' He practically purrs the words, savouring them. 'All you wanted was someone to love you. So I pretended to and you fell for it. I knew that if I let you think how damaged I was, you'd want to fix it. I can read you like a book. A simple one, at that.'

Each word twists like a knife in my gut. 'So you never loved me?' My voice breaks. 'This – our relationship – was nothing but a game to you?'

'I'm a great actor. You two women should know that,' Tom drawls, looking between me and Vivienne with a perverted satisfaction shining from his eyes. His lips curl into a sneer. 'You both need to understand that I hate you. I've never loved either of you. Everything I did was a means to an end, and that was to destroy you, Vivienne. To make you suffer like I did. And I didn't care how long it took.'

'But why me, when I've never done anything to hurt you?' I ask, hardly believing the words he's uttering.

'I needed someone to help me and you fit the bill: a vulnerable, easily manipulated, not very bright woman.'

My mind flashes to Lola – Vivienne's precious daughter – and bile rises in my throat at the thought of how he's hurt them both. Guilt for what I've done to them coursing through me.

'What about your daughter? How could you do this to a child?' I ask.

He shrugs. 'Let's just call her collateral damage.' His eyes glitter with malice.

The weight of Tom's betrayal suddenly crashes over me like a physical wave. How could I not have noticed?

Every memory from our past shifts and warps, taking on totally different meanings. All those times he'd talked about his troubled childhood, and how he hated the girl who'd accused his father and caused him to take his own life... it wasn't because he wanted my support and sympathy. It was to make sure I'd help him destroy Vivienne.

'How did you even find me? Why now?' Vivienne's question cuts through my spiralling thoughts, sharp as a blade.

'It wasn't hard.' He's practically preening now, proud of his deception. 'After a night of online drunken stalking, I came across some school-reunion photos and saw you. It wasn't hard to find out where you lived and to make sure I *bumped* into you.' His smile is chilling. 'You were ripe for the picking, desperate for someone to love you and your kid.'

'But you said Amelia was recommended to you by a colleague – you must have known what she was going to do?' Vivienne says.

'It was all part of the plan.'

'Well, now we know what you've done, I'm going to the police.' Vivienne's voice is like steel as she pulls out her phone.

The room falls silent except for the sound of my own ragged breaths. My entire life with Tom is crumbling away, and in the rubble stands a stranger. A monster wearing my partner's face.

FORTY-TWO

VIVIENNE

Cold panic grips me as I fumble with the phone, my thumb sliding uselessly across the numbers while trying to press 999 to call the police.

'Don't you dare,' Miles snarls, his face dark with rage. Before I can react, he lunges at me with frightening speed, his shoes squeaking against the kitchen tiles.

I stumble backwards, my hip catching the corner of the island, and yelp in pain as it shoots through my side. I clutch my phone like a lifeline. 'Stay back,' I yell.

Willow charges into the kitchen at the sound of my voice, her bark echoing off the walls as she rushes over to protect me. My brave girl. But Miles's face twists with contempt as he kicks her aside, his boot connecting with her ribs. Her yelp of pain tears through me as she crashes into the kitchen cabinets.

'Willow,' I try to scream, but suddenly Miles is on me, his hands wrapped around my throat. My phone clatters to the floor, skidding across the tiles. I claw at his fingers, my nails drawing blood, but he doesn't even flinch. He's too strong.

'You had this coming,' he hisses, his face inches from mine. His breath is hot against my skin, smelling of coffee and rage.

His eyes are empty now, devoid of anything human. 'You ruined my life, killing the people I loved. Now it's your turn to die.'

I kick out, my knee connecting with his thigh, but it's like hitting concrete. His thumbs press deeper into my windpipe, crushing the air out of me. My teeth clench as I try to twist away, and my body writhes against the kitchen counter. Something clatters to the floor – a mug, maybe, or a plate. The sound seems distant now.

Black spots dance at the edges of my vision as I gasp for air. My lungs burn like I've swallowed fire. My hand slips from his wrist, falling uselessly to my side. I try to raise it again but can't.

Lola's face flashes before my eyes – her sweet smile, the way she looked this afternoon in her new pink dress when I took her to the party, her blonde hair catching the sunlight. *Oh God, Lola.* Who will collect her? Who will tell her that Mummy's never coming home?

The thought of her waiting at the party, watching all the other children leave with their parents, makes me summon one last burst of energy. I slam my palm up into Miles's chin... but it's weak and uncoordinated.

His grip only tightens in response.

Lola can't lose me. She's only five. Who will hold her when she has nightmares? Who will know that she likes her special blue cup for hot chocolate, or that Mr Snuggles needs to be tucked in just right? I thrash harder, my shoulder blades scraping against the counter, but my strength is fading like water down a drain.

My mouth opens and closes uselessly, like a fish on land. The fluorescent kitchen lights blur above me, too bright, too harsh. I think of Lola's birthday coming up. The presents I've hidden in my wardrobe and the cake I ordered with the unicorn on top. Will anyone even know to cancel it?

The edges of the room grow fuzzy and dark. My right hand drops completely, fingers brushing against the cabinet handle.

My baby, my precious girl… I'm so sorry. I'm so sorry I won't be there to see you grow up.

But then, through my darkening vision, I catch a flash of movement behind Miles. My oxygen-starved brain takes a moment to process what I'm seeing through the tears clouding my eyes.

It's Amelia.

She's standing there, trembling but determined, a kitchen knife clutched in her hand. The overhead lights catch the blade, making it gleam. Her face is a mask of horror and resolve, and I know in that moment that everything's about to change.

Please, I think desperately, though I don't know if I'm praying to Amelia, or God, or anyone who might listen. Please let me live. My daughter needs me.

Through the roaring in my ears, I hear Willow whimper from somewhere on the floor. The sound grows fainter as consciousness slips away, but I keep my eyes fixed on Amelia. On the knife. On my last hope.

FORTY-THREE

AMELIA

I stare at the knife in my shaky hand, its weight unfamiliar and terrifying. The metal handle is cold against my palm and it's already slick with sweat. Time seems to go into slow motion as I watch Tom's fingers dig deeper into Vivienne's throat, his fingers rigid with effort. Her face is turning purple and her eyes are bulging as she claws desperately at his hands, trying to make him stop. The sound of her choking fills the kitchen, mixing with the hum of the fluorescent lights and my own thundering heartbeat.

I open my mouth to speak, but the words stick in my throat like glass shards.

This isn't my Tom. It's someone else. Someone I don't know. The realisation hits me like a physical blow, making my knees weak. This isn't the man who knows exactly how I like my tea and who can make me laugh, even on my darkest days. This isn't the man I thought I knew, the man I trusted, the man I... *No.* This is a stranger wearing his face, a monster who's been hiding behind gentle smiles and soft touches. He used me, just like he used Vivienne. Every moment together – every kiss, every whispered promise – they were all lies.

Every time he said 'I love you', he was really saying 'You're such a fool.'

The kitchen light catches the blade in my hand, sending reflections dancing across the walls. They remind me of the way sunlight used to play across Tom's face in the morning, but that memory feels poisoned now, tainted by the truth. Was he thinking about this moment even then? Was everything just a calculated step towards this violence? Towards ending the life of the person he hates most in the world?

Vivienne's struggles are getting weaker. Her arms are loose by her side, and I know she only has seconds left unless I do something. If I let him kill her, I'll be next. That much is obvious. There won't be anyone left to tell the truth about what he's done.

The weight of responsibility crashes down on me. Vivienne's life, her daughter's future, my own survival are all balanced on this knife's edge.

I must do something. I can't stand here and watch her die. Watch Tom kill her for something that wasn't her fault. I know that now.

I have to do it now, before it's too late.

But I'm not a violent person. I've never even been in a fight before.

It doesn't matter. This is different. I must put an end to this.

With a sickening lurch of my stomach, I pull back the knife and plunge it hard into his back. The resistance of flesh and muscle is nothing like in the movies. It takes more force than I expect, and the sound... Oh God, the sound... Like punching through wet cardboard, but softer, more organic. As the blade slides between his ribs, I realise with horrible certainty that I've done what I needed to.

Tom's grip on Vivienne's throat loosens instantly. He jerks backwards, the knife sliding out as he turns to face me, his eyes widening at the sight of the bloodied blade still gripped in my hand. For a split second, I see Tom there – my Tom – in the way his brow furrows in confusion, the same expression he wears when he can't find his keys. The Tom I'll always love.

My heart shatters all over again as he falls to the floor, blood pooling around him in an ever-widening circle. The crimson spreads across the kitchen tiles like spilled wine, but darker and much thicker.

I stand over Tom and he lets out a low groan. The bloody knife is still clutched tight in my hand. My fingers are unable to release the handle; it's as if they've frozen around it. Crimson drops fall from the blade, splattering against the tiles like rain. My eyes meet with Tom's, and in that moment, I see everything. His surprise, betrayal, anger and fear. He opens his mouth as if to speak, but no words come out. He stops moving and his eyes go vacant. He's dead.

The copper smell of blood fills my nostrils, mixing with the lingering scent of his aftershave. The one I bought him for Christmas after he said how much he loved it. My stomach heaves at the combination.

The man I love and the monster he's become blur together in my vision, making it impossible to separate.

What have I done?

PART FOUR

THE FALLOUT

FORTY-FOUR

VIVIENNE

I stare at Miles's body, lifeless on the kitchen floor, my vision swimming as the reality of what just happened crashes over me. My gaze shifts to Amelia, who's standing like a statue with the bloody knife in her hand. When our eyes meet, I see my own shock and horror reflected back at me. In that moment, a silent understanding passes between us. We're both victims and survivors of this grotesque nightmare.

'What have I done?' Amelia whispers, her voice cracking.

'You saved my life.' The words feel inadequate against the weight of everything that's passed between us. 'Thank you, Amelia. Thank you.'

'But what do we do now?' Amelia asks. Her hand is shaking badly, but the knife remains firmly grasped between her fingers.

'Put that down,' I say quickly, gesturing to the knife. 'We don't want any more accidents.'

Amelia stares, wide-eyed, at the blade, as if seeing it for the first time and lets it clatter to the floor. She stumbles backwards, leaning against the island. 'Oh God, oh God...'

As if moving on autopilot, I run into the utility room, grab one of Willow's towels and lay it over Miles. I can't bear to look at his face – the face that smiled at me so many times while hiding such unimaginable darkness.

I catch sight of Willow cowering in the corner and rush to her side, my heart aching at her fear. 'Hey, it's okay,' I murmur, holding out a treat. She inches toward me and settles by my side, leaning into me while I stroke and comfort her. Her warm presence is oddly consoling in this surreal moment.

'I think we need to go into the garden and talk this through,' I say to Amelia after a few moments. I'm surprised by how steady my voice sounds, when inside it feels like I'm falling apart.

'Are we going to leave him there on the floor?' Amelia asks, nodding at Miles's covered body.

'For now. We need some fresh air and time to think clearly.' I take her arm gently. 'Come with me.'

I lead her outside, and we sink into my new wicker garden furniture that I only bought a few weeks ago. The normality of it feels strangely absurd, given what's happened inside.

The afternoon air is mild and birds are singing. It seems impossible that the world can continue so normally when our lives have changed immeasurably. Forever.

'So now what?' Amelia asks, wrapping her arms around her knees and rocking gently. She's clearly in shock.

I take a deep breath, trying to organise my scattered thoughts. 'I think we need to agree we're both victims of Miles... or Tom... I don't even know what his real name is.'

It's surreal to be talking about him like this. But I can't allow myself to give in to the enormity of what's happened. At least not now. There's too much that needs sorting out for me to give in to that.

'Yes, we both are,' Amelia acknowledges, her face pale. 'But now he's dead. And I killed him.' Her voice rises, and she sounds verging on hysteria.

'Shh,' I caution, glancing at the neighbouring houses,

hoping that we can't be heard. 'Listen to me, Amelia. You acted in self-defence, over me *and* you. He was going to kill me. And most likely you'd have been next. I mean, we both witnessed what he was capable of when pushed. I have no doubt that if you hadn't killed him first, it would be the two of us lying dead on the floor.'

'But will the police believe us?' Amelia's eyes fill with tears. 'Two women, both involved with the same man, and one of us kills him... Who would believe it wasn't planned after we found out how he'd been playing us both? If I was an outsider, I'd think his death was premeditated.'

'What about the bruising on my neck, surely that would be enough to corroborate our story,' I say.

'Or they might think we killed him because he was abusing you as well as seeing me,' Amelia countered.

She's right. It could look like a conspiracy and that we plotted our revenge together after discovering his deception and then his attack on me. I run my hands through my hair and let out a frustrated sigh.

'Look, we need to think about the future. Miles, Tom, whatever is gone now. He won't be coming back. We're the most important people now. And Lola, of course. We have to think about her.'

Amelia's face drains of what little colour it had left. 'Oh my goodness, I forgot about Lola. What are you going to tell her?'

'She's at a party at the moment,' I remind her, my mind racing through options. 'I'll phone one of her friends' parents and ask if they can pick her up and keep her at their house for a while? I'll say I've been held up in a traffic jam. There are always holdups around here, so it won't appear suspicious.'

'Okay. Yes. That's a good idea. Do it now,' Amelia says.

While I head inside to collect my phone, my mind tries to process what's happened and the best way to deal with it. All I can come up with is that we must cover up Miles's death and dispose of a body. The very thought of it makes me feel sick... like I'm in some terrible crime drama. But what choice do we have? The alternative will destroy three lives. Mine, Lola's and Amelia's.

I make the call and then return outside. Amelia is sitting quietly staring ahead, looking slightly calmer than when I left her.

I sit down next to her. 'I've made the call, which means we have a couple of hours to deal with everything. This is my plan.' I swallow hard, my throat tight. 'I never thought I'd hear myself saying this, but we must cover up Miles's death. Because if not, the consequences are too dire. We need to protect each other.'

'You mean... hide the body?' Amelia looks horrified. 'That's... that's a serious crime. Concealing a death, interfering with a corpse...' She starts breathing faster. 'We could go to prison just for that, without even considering the murder.'

I must remain calm, because it's clear Amelia is close to the edge and we can't afford for that to happen.

'The alternative is far worse, Amelia,' I say softly, even though my stomach's churning. 'Think about it logically. The best-case scenario is the police believe it was self-defence. But even so, our lives will still be ruined. Can you imagine how the media will play it? They'll have a field day. "Love Rival Kills Two-Timing Pilot." Or something equally melodramatic. Lola would never recover from that kind of publicity. It would follow her right through school. And then there's the worst-case scenario, which is they don't believe us, and we both go down for murder and Lola is put in care. Do you understand?'

I have no choice but to lay it on thick like this because Amelia needs to realise what we're facing.

'I do,' Amelia says, nodding slowly. 'But how are we going to get rid of Tom without anyone worrying where he is and becoming suspicious?'

I lean forward, forcing myself to think rationally despite the chaos in my mind. 'We need to find out more about Miles... or Tom. He said he worked for the army as a civilian pilot but was that the truth?'

'For me, he was a consultant project manager. I think that was true because of all the phone conversations he had regarding work and I'd see some of his work in his study. He went away sometimes, which must have been when he came home to you,' Amelia says, her brow furrowing. 'He must have lied to you about being a pilot.'

'It was the perfect cover story, especially as he told me he was doing top-secret work,' I say bitterly.

'I imagine then that the name Miles was made up,' Amelia says.

'No, Miles was his middle name. He said his name was Tyrone Miles Clarke, but always went by Miles. His surname should have been Williams, if Mr Williams was his father. Unless he changed his name after he was put in care so he couldn't be traced.'

'But you're not Clarke,' Amelia says.

'No. I kept my maiden name, Campbell. Because we met later in life, it would have been a nightmare to change everything. It all makes sense now. He told me his real name began with a *T*, which meant I wasn't going to query any bank statements or anything coming in for T. M. Clarke. For you, he's also T. Clarke.'

'And because I only knew your surname, I didn't think anything was strange.'

'He might not have thought it through properly,' I say with a sigh. 'I could've told you his surname during our meetings... but then, we still might not have twigged...'

'This is completely insane,' Amelia whispers. 'We're sitting here planning... planning...' She can't finish the sentence.

'I know,' I say softly. 'But we must stay focused and think

this through carefully. One mistake and...' I don't need to finish the sentence.

We sit there in silence for a while, the weight of our situation pressing down on us. Then an idea forms in my mind. It's crazy, but it should work. My heart thumps in my ears.

'Can you find out the projects Tom was working on, and ones he had lined up?'

'I think so. Why?' Amelia asks, uncertainty written across her face.

'We need to phone the clients and tell them he's had a stroke and that he'll be unable to finish the projects he's working on. If he owes them any money, then we can reimburse them.'

'And then what do we do?' Amelia's voice is barely audible.

I force myself to say the words we're both dreading. 'We have to dispose of the body.'

Amelia gasps, her hand flying to her mouth. For a moment, I think she might be sick. 'I can't... I can't believe we're talking about this,' she manages finally. 'It's like we're in some horrible nightmare.'

I reach out and squeeze her hand. 'I know, but we must be practical now. I've got some tarpaulins in the garage. Between us—'

'But where?' she interrupts, her voice wobbly. 'Where could we possibly... Oh God, I can't even say it.'

'I'm not sure yet.' I try to sound more confident than I feel.

'But people might come looking for him,' Amelia says.

'I don't think they will,' I say slowly. 'Looking back, since we've been together, he's never had any close friends. It was also just the two of us. This is my house, and he was never put on the mortgage, so him disappearing won't make a difference. If anyone asks, I'll say he's left me. What about for you? Did Tom ever have friends around?'

'Well, no, it was the same for us.'

'Down the track, if anyone contacts you and asks about him,

you can say that he's moved into a nursing home. I don't think they will. I think he was so wrapped up in manipulating the two of us, he couldn't afford to let anybody else in.' My voice turns bitter. 'That should work in our favour.'

'Are we really going to do this?' Amelia asks, her voice barely audible. 'There's no going back once we start.'

I look at her steadily. 'We've already started. The moment that knife went in, our lives changed forever. Now we have to decide what version of forever we're going to live with.'

She nods, and the same grim determination I'm feeling settles over her features. We're two ordinary women planning something extraordinary... something terrible.

But sometimes survival requires terrible things. And right now, survival is all we have.

FORTY-FIVE

AMELIA

Sunday

I spend the day at home, unable to leave. The walls of my house feel both suffocating and protective. But now, standing at Vivienne's front door Sunday evening, my heart is pounding with anxiety. I know we can't do anything until Lola goes to bed, but I couldn't stand being alone with my thoughts anymore.

I ring the doorbell, my hand shaking slightly. Each second of waiting feels like an eternity.

The door opens, and Vivienne greets me with a forced smile. 'Hi.'

I start to frown, then notice Lola beside her and understand the pretence. My stomach churns with guilt – the poor kid has no idea what we've done.

'Hello,' I manage. 'How are you, Lola?' I ask, looking down into the girl's innocent brown eyes.

'Mummy let me stay up late until you were here so you can read me a bedtime story.' Lola beams.

I swallow hard, remembering my promise. How on earth am I going to manage that?

'Yeah, great,' I say.

'I hope you don't mind,' Vivienne says. 'Come in while I'm getting Lola's lunch ready for tomorrow. Lola, you can watch your cartoon for a bit longer and then we'll go upstairs.'

Luckily, Lola agrees and we head through to the kitchen.

'Are you okay?' I ask.

'It all seems so surreal,' Vivienne says. 'How are you?'

'I didn't sleep at all last night,' I admit.

Vivienne sighs and nods. 'Me neither, knowing what we're about to do.'

We both know what she means. This evening, after it gets dark, is when we're going to bury the body that's currently in her garage.

Willow comes over and settles beside me, as if sensing my distress, and I give her a pat.

After Vivienne has made the lunch, we collect Lola and go upstairs. Somehow I manage to read the story she wants – something about a unicorn – and then I go back to the lounge and watch the telly with Vivienne until it begins to get dark.

'Okay, let's do this,' she says grimly.

I don't move from the couch. My body feels impossibly heavy, as if gravity itself has increased overnight. 'I've been thinking about it all last night and today,' I confess, my voice barely above a whisper. My throat constricts around the words I never imagined I'd speak. 'That my Tom – your Miles – is wrapped up in your garage...' The reality of it hits me again, a physical pain behind my ribs. 'What if...?'

'Nobody's been in there.' Vivienne's practical tone anchors me somewhat. Her eyes, though rimmed with exhaustion, remain clear and focused. It's both comforting and terrifying how steadily she's handling this. 'We'll go into the garden and measure how deep the well is before we do anything else.'

I stand by the kitchen door that leads to the garage and watch Vivienne pick up a measuring tape from a work bench and two spades. Her movements are precise, methodical. She's never struck me as being like this. Has the crisis transformed her into this efficient stranger before me?

We go out of the door from the garage into the garden, walking down to the far corner where the well's situated. Luckily it's out of the neighbours' eyesight.

'You seem so calm,' I observe, studying her side profile as she concentrates on lowering the tape down the well.

'I'm not,' she admits, giving a quick glance in my direction. Something flickers across her face – fear, grief, I can't tell anymore. 'I just know that if I let this get to me...'

Her words hang in the air. I understand what she can't say. If we let ourselves feel it – truly feel what we've done – we'll shatter into pieces too small to ever put back together.

Vivienne leans over the low fence and drops the measuring tape down the well. It unspools for what seems like ages, metal clicking against stone as it descends into darkness. I find myself holding my breath, as if the well might somehow reject our plan, prove too shallow for our terrible purpose.

'Have you reached the bottom yet?' I ask as the tape runs out. My voice sounds strange, too high, too brittle.

'Not yet, which means it's over thirty feet.' Vivienne's mouth curves into something that's not quite a smile. 'Which is perfect for what we want.'

Perfect. Such an obscene word for this moment. But I nod anyway, feeling a terrible relief wash over me. The well's deep enough to swallow our sins. Deep enough that no one will ever find the remains of the man we once loved... once feared... once killed.

'Now what?' I ask.

Vivienne hands me a spade. 'We need to dig up enough earth to cover the body, in case anyone peers down into the well when the landscaper arrives to cover it over.'

'Have you already arranged something?'

'I have someone coming tomorrow.' She stares into the darkness of the well, shoulders slumping slightly. 'I'm going to cover it with decking and make a play area for Lola.'

I stare at Vivienne, searching her face. The exhaustion is finally breaking through her calm facade. 'Are you sure? Do you really want Lola to be playing on top of where a body's buried?'

Her eyes widen, as if she's only now hearing her own words. She presses a trembling hand to her mouth. 'God, what am I thinking? I'm not...'

'Concrete it over and then put a raised vegetable bed on top?' I suggest gently. 'Something useful but not... a place for children.'

'Yes, that could work. Thanks.' She draws a shaky breath. 'It's like part of me is on autopilot. I wasn't thinking straight.'

I reach for her hand, surprised by my own gesture of comfort. 'Neither of us are.'

We begin digging from the grassed area that runs along the rear of the garden, making a pile of dirt that seems to mock our efforts. Each spadeful of earth seems to weigh more than the last, the resistance of the soil matching the heaviness in my chest. The pile appears alarmingly small despite our concerted efforts, as if the ground itself is reluctant to make space for what we're about to do. Sweat runs down my back in rivulets and my hands are starting to blister.

'This can't be real,' I whisper, more to myself than to Vivienne.

All I can think of is how this place will become Tom's secret resting place. No headstone, no mourners, just anonymous earth and our guilty knowledge of where he lies. The thought makes my stomach lurch.

'I think this is enough,' Vivienne finally says when the mound is quite big. Her face is streaked with dirt and tears. Her eyes meet mine, hollow with shock. 'Let's bring him out.'

My heart hammers so hard I fear it might break through my ribs. I nod, unable to form any words.

We leave our spades on the ground and head back to the garage. The walk feels both endless and too short. Vivienne's car is in there, innocuous and ordinary, a vehicle that has carried shopping, suitcases, and now... this. She opens the back to reveal the body wrapped in a blue tarpaulin. The plastic gleams unnaturally bright in the dim garage light.

'I can't believe—' I start, but choke on the words.

Vivienne grips my arm, her fingers digging into my flesh. 'We have to,' she whispers fiercely. 'There's no going back.'

With all our strength, muscles screaming in protest, we pull him out and drag him out of the garage door. The tarpaulin snags on the gravel, and I bite back a hysterical laugh. Even in death, Tom is making things difficult.

Down to the well we go, each step an eternity. We push him over the small, bricked wall circling it, and the blue bundle disappears into darkness.

After a couple of seconds, there's a sickening thud when he hits the bottom. The sound will haunt my nightmares forever, I'm certain. My legs nearly buckle beneath me. I turn to Vivienne, bile rising in my throat.

'That's it then,' I manage to say, the words hollow and inadequate for the enormity of what we've done.

She nods, her face a mask of grim determination beneath the shock. Then she picks up the spade and begins shovelling the earth we'd dug up into the well. I follow suit, each shovelful of dirt landing with a soft pattering sound that feels like an accusation.

'By the way, I found this in his wallet,' Vivienne suddenly says, her voice oddly detached as she drops the spade onto the ground and pulls out a folded newspaper article from her pocket.

My dirty hands leave smudges of earth along the creases as I take it from her, the paper yellow with age and handling. I unfold it carefully. The headline swims before my eyes, then comes into sharp, terrible focus.

I read it and my blood runs cold, a glacial chill spreading from my core to my fingertips as the horror of his past collides with the horror of his present – of what we've done – and for a moment, I can't breathe.

The Daily Echo

Tragedy Strikes Again: Son of Accused Teacher Loses Mother, Enters Foster Care

March 10, 1996

In a heartbreaking turn of events, the eleven-year-old son of the late James Williams, who the court has decided should not have his first name published, has been placed in foster care following the death of his mother, Sarah Williams, 42. The family has been in the public eye since last September when James Williams, a secondary-school teacher, took his own life after being accused of sexually assaulting a student.

Friends and neighbours reported that Sarah had been struggling to cope with the loss of her husband and the stigma surrounding the accusations against him. 'She was a shell of her former self,' said a close family friend. 'She loved James so much, and she just couldn't bear the thought of him being guilty of something so horrible.'

Despite the support of the community, Sarah's mental health continued to deteriorate. She was found deceased in her home last week, with the cause of death being ruled as an accidental overdose of prescription medication.

With no other family members able to take custody, her young son has been placed in the care of the social services. When questioned, social workers have assured the public that they will do everything in their power to ensure the boy receives the support and care he needs during this difficult time.

The tragedy has reignited discussions about the impact of such accusations on families of an accused. 'It's so sad,' said a neighbour who wished to remain anonymous. 'That poor boy has lost both his parents, and his life will never be the same.'

The Williamses' story serves as a poignant reminder of the far-reaching consequences of such allegations and the importance of supporting all those affected by these tragedies.

As for the young boy, the community can only hope that he will find the strength and resilience to overcome these hardships and build a better future for himself.

'That tells us everything then, doesn't it?' I say, the pieces finally clicking into place. 'I get why he did it, but him manipulating me and you from the start...' I shake my head, remembering. A cold shudder runs through me as the full extent of his deception sinks in. 'I don't get how he persuaded me to go after you, or at least how he made me think it was my idea.'

'He was an expert at manipulation. That's how.' Vivienne's eyes darken as she absorbs the truth. 'But how did you manage to get this housesitting job?'

'It was Tom's idea that I should housesit for you. One day he came home from work really upset. He said he'd been overseeing some work at this beautiful house and that it turned out to be yours. He said you didn't recognise him because he was only eleven when it all happened with his dad. He told me that you weren't struggling like we were and that it wasn't fair you had such a perfect life and we didn't. He said all you had to worry about was finding a dogsitter.'

'And then he suggested you should do the job?'

'No, he was cleverer than that. I said to him that your life probably wasn't as perfect as it seems and that maybe I should housesit to prove that to him. I didn't really mean it, but he then jumped on the idea and put my details on the site. He even said that doing it might help him put his traumatic past behind him and we could try for a baby. I'm so sorry.'

'He was a monster and played us both. Don't apologise.'

'No, I have to. Because then I took matters into my own hands.' Tears start falling, and I can't stop them. 'He didn't ask me to do those things to you. It was my idea, because I thought he'd be pleased once I'd succeeded in...' A sob escapes my lips. 'I'm so sorry. Please forgive me.'

'It's not your fault,' Vivienne says gently. 'You wouldn't have done it if it wasn't for him cleverly manipulating you. You did very well because you certainly had me believing that I was totally losing the plot.'

'I'm sorry,' I repeat, meaning it.

'It's over now...' Vivienne's voice trails off as we both stare at the well. 'What happened is our secret. And it's now literally buried.'

We stand in silence. Two women bound together by a terrible secret. The well before us seems bottomless – a dark mirror of the truth we now share. Will we ever feel clean again?

I glance at Vivienne and see my own complicated future reflected in her eyes. We're strangers who know each other's darkest moment. Whatever comes next, we'll carry this weight together.

EPILOGUE

VIVIENNE

Three months later

'Mummy. Auntie Milly. Look at me.'

I glance across at the swings, watching Lola as she pumps her legs, managing to swing herself higher and higher. Her innocent laughter fills the air, and for a moment, it pushes back the darkness that still threatens to overwhelm me. Thankfully, my daughter is untouched by the weight of what happened that day.

I turn to Milly – I can't think of her as Amelia anymore; she's become so much more than that stranger who appeared in my life a few months ago – and watch as she, too, observes my daughter. The same mix of emotions I'm feeling is playing across her face. Joy at Lola's happiness, guilt at our deception, relief that we've managed to protect her from the truth.

We share a look, a silent acknowledgement of the bond that now ties us together. The secret we carry is like a thread between us, invisible but unbreakable.

'You're doing so well, darling,' I call out to Lola.

'Yes, you are,' Milly echoes, her voice warm with genuine affection. 'Almost as high as last time.'

'Higher,' Lola shouts back, determined as ever.

Milly leans closer to me on the bench. 'The school secretary asked about him again yesterday when I picked her up.'

My stomach tightens. 'What did you say?'

'I stuck to our story, as agreed. I told her that he'd walked out on you and left no forwarding address.'

'Good,' I acknowledge with a nod. 'And it's not like he's Lola's real father, so they have no reason to find him. Have you heard anything from his past clients?'

'No. I think he made out he was more in demand than he really was.'

We sit in silence for a few minutes, absorbed in our thoughts.

'Ice cream van,' Milly says suddenly. 'Shall I...?'

'Would you mind?' I ask. 'Her usual...'

'Strawberry swirl with sprinkles,' Milly finishes with a smile.

She knows all of Lola's favourites now.

As I watch her walk towards the ice cream van, I remember how this new normal developed. It started with Milly coming over almost every evening after that day, both of us too scared to be alone with our thoughts. She helped with Lola, and then we'd have dinner once Lola was asleep, and after we'd sit in silence, or sometimes talk about everything and nothing, providing it wasn't about what had happened.

Nightmares plagued both of us. There were nights when one of us would call the other at three in the morning, gasping and crying. We developed a code: 'I can't sleep' meant 'I'm seeing his face again' or 'I can smell the earth' or 'I keep feeling the weight of him.'

'Look how high I can go,' Lola shouts.

'Be careful, sweetheart,' I call back, my heart swelling with love for her.

Milly returns with the ice creams, and Lola runs over, her cheeks flushed with excitement.

'Thank you, Auntie Milly.' She throws her arms around Milly's waist, and I see Milly's eyes grow wet.

'You're welcome, darling,' Milly says softly. 'After we've eaten these, shall we show Mummy the special dance we've been practising?'

'That's a great idea,' I say.

This is new – their secret ballet sessions in the living room while I'm cooking dinner. Milly used to dance, she told us, and now she's teaching Lola. I watch as they twirl together on the grass and feel a rush of gratitude for this strange new family we've become.

'I've been thinking,' Milly says later as Lola feeds the ducks. 'Maybe I should look at the house for rent around the corner from you. I don't want to stay where I am.'

I look at her, surprised. We've talked in abstract terms about living closer together. It started as a joke, but lately…

'It has three bedrooms,' Milly continues carefully. 'Which means Lola can stay over with me any time she wants, if you'll let her.'

'What will you do with your house?'

'Sell it. There won't be much money left after the mortgage has been paid, and I can forge Tom's signature on all the documents.'

'It's a big step. Are you sure?'

'I'm sure I hate where I am. And this way…' She doesn't finish, but I understand. This way, we'd be close enough to keep each other sane and keep our secret together.

'In that case, I think it's a great idea and I'm sure Lola would love it.'

Lola asked about Miles for a while, but because she was

used to him not being around much anyway, she seemed to accept it when I told her that Daddy had gone away for a long time. Milly and I had decided to stick to something like we'd told other people because it seemed safer that way.

Lola comes racing over to us, closely followed by the dog.

'Can I throw the ball for Willow?' Lola asks, giving the dog a stroke.

'Here you are,' I say, pulling a tennis ball from my pocket and handing it to her. 'But don't go too far. I want you in my eyesight at all times.'

'Yes, Mummy,' Lola says, with a roll of her eyes.

Sometimes she reminds me so much of Miles, which is weird because he was only her stepfather. I guess some of his mannerisms rubbed off on her. But I can't go down that path. It's way too difficult.

Last week, we finally cleared out his things from my house. Milly helped me box everything up and we drove them to a charity shop over an hour away.

'Lola, not too far,' I call out as I see her heading further and further away.

'I'll go,' Milly says, jumping up to follow her. She's so protective of Lola now, as if making up for something that wasn't her fault to begin with.

I watch them together, my daughter and the woman who should have been my enemy but has now become my best friend. Milly's teaching Lola to braid her hair and showing her how to tend the little herb garden we started last month. Sometimes I hear them giggling together over books or making up stories about the clouds.

The future stretches out before us, uncertain but full of possibility. Work is going well, and I'm thinking of applying for promotion. Lola is thriving in school and her teachers have commented on how well she's adjusting.

The guilt will never completely leave me, I know that.

Sometimes I wake in the night, remembering the weight of the spade in my hands and the smell of fresh earth. But then I remember I would have been dead if not for Milly. There was no other way the situation could have ended.

'Mummy, come on,' Lola calls. 'Come and play with us.'

I jump up and head towards what is now my family. The sun is warm on my face and ahead of me, Lola's laughter mingles with the sound of quacking ducks and Milly's gentle voice.

Last night, I found a note from Lola on my pillow. *I love you, Mummy and Auntie Milly*, written in wobbly letters with a crayon heart. I showed it to Milly this morning, and we both cried a little. Not from guilt this time, but from hope.

We're going to be okay. And maybe that's enough.

As I reach them, Lola grabs both our hands, swinging between us. 'Can we get pizza for dinner?'

'I think we can manage that,' Milly says, looking at me.

I nod, squeezing both of their hands. 'Pizza and movie night?'

'Yes.' Lola cheers. 'Can we watch *Frozen* again?'

'Again?' I groan, but I'm smiling.

'Please?' Lola and Milly say together, and I laugh.

This is our life now. Pizza and Disney movies, secret dances and herb gardens, shared nightmares and healing hugs. Not perfect and not what any of us planned. But it's ours. And as I watch my daughter teaching Milly our special handshake, I know that sometimes family is what you make it.

A LETTER FROM THE AUTHOR

Dear reader,

Huge thanks for reading *The Silent Guest*. If you want to join other readers in hearing all about my new releases and bonus content, you can sign up here:

www.stormpublishing.co/sally-rigby

If you enjoyed this book and could spare a few moments to leave a review that would be hugely appreciated. Even a short review can make all the difference in encouraging a reader to discover my books for the first time. Thank you so much.

I chose to write about a housesitter because I find their situation fascinating. They're trusted to live in someone's home but still an outsider. For a psychological thriller, it's a brilliant setup for paranoia and discovering secrets.

Thanks again for being part of this amazing journey with me and I hope you'll stay in touch – I have so many more stories and ideas to entertain you with.

Sally Rigby

www.sallyrigby.com

facebook.com/Sally-Rigby-131414630527848

ACKNOWLEDGEMENTS

I would like to express my sincere thanks to all the people who helped bring *The Silent Guest* to life.

First, my friend Amanda Ashby deserves special recognition. The endless brainstorming was invaluable and her insistence that one should always 'add one more twist' is constantly at the back of my mind.

My gratitude also extends to everyone at Storm Publishing who contributed to this book. Kathryn Taussig, thank you for all your insightful editorial guidance and for taking a chance on this manuscript. I'm also grateful to the editing staff for their careful attention to detail and helpful suggestions that strengthened the story. Thanks to the talented cover designer who created such a striking visual for the book, and to the marketing team for their efforts in connecting this novel with readers.

To my family, thanks, as always, for all your understanding and encouragement.

Printed in Dunstable, United Kingdom

72872123R10143